Mr. Malcolm's List

'Suz   Allain delivers a fresh and spirited take on the cla   Regency romp. *Mr. Malcolm's List* is a delightful t   that perfectly illustrates the enduring appeal of the Regency romance. It's all here—the fast, witty banter, the elegant ballrooms, the quirky characters, the charming, strong-willed heroine and the dashing hero who has a thing or two to learn about love'

—*New York Times* bestselling author Amanda Quick

'A merry romp! *Mr. Malcolm's List* is packed with action as one tangled romantic misunderstanding follows fast upon another's heels—to hilarious effect'

—*New York Times* bestselling author Mary Balogh

'Suzanne Allain is a fresh new voice in historical romance. *Mr. Malcolm's List* is a charming, lighthearted confection, with humour, sparkling banter, and gently simmering romantic tension; in other words, classic Regency romance'

—Nation   nne Gracie

Mr. Malcolm's List

SUZANNE ALLAIN

PIATKUS

PIATKUS

First published in the US in 2020 by Jove, Berkley
An imprint of Penguin Random House LLC
First published in Great Britain in 2020 by Piatkus

Originally self-published, in different form, in 2009

1 3 5 7 9 10 8 6 4 2

A CIP catalogue record for this book
is available from the British Library.

ISBN 978-0-349-42756-0

Printed and bound in Great Britain by Clays Ltd, Elcograf S.p.A.

Papers used by Piatkus are from well-managed forests
and other responsible sources.

Piatkus
An imprint of
Little, Brown Book Group
Carmelite House
50 Victoria Embankment
London EC4Y 0DZ

An Hachette UK Company
www.hachette.co.uk

www.littlebrown.co.uk

For my husband
A very fastidious gentleman who made an excellent choice

1

The Honorable Jeremy Malcolm, second son of the Earl of Kilbourne, was the biggest catch of the season the year of our Lord 1818. It was true he had no title of his own and was only a younger son, but his aunt on his mother's side had left him the bulk of her sizeable fortune and a large country house in Kent.

He also had his considerable personal assets to recommend him. Only the most ambitious of young misses would overlook the handsome Mr. Malcolm in favor of the Marquess of Mumford, who was at least fifty and had no chin, just for the privilege of hearing herself called "my lady."

For what woman would choose to be called "my lady" when she might enjoy the sole honor of being called "Malcolm's lady"?

But it was beginning to look as if no woman was ever to enjoy that inestimable privilege.

For, though he was by no means a hermit, and attended Almack's along with various other balls, routs, and assemblies, Mr. Malcolm was earning a reputation as a Trifler, a Breaker of Hearts, a Destroyer of Young Ladies' Dreams.

"A what?" Malcolm asked his friend Lord Cassidy, upon being told of the latest gossip concerning him.

"A Destroyer of Young Ladies' Dreams," Cassie told him, enunciating slowly and carefully.

"What rot," Malcolm replied, turning to survey the ballroom, and one beautiful debutante in particular.

"Perhaps the gossips are correct. You paid very particular attentions to my cousin Julia, and now have not been to call in over a week."

Malcolm turned to look at his friend, one eyebrow raised. "I escorted your cousin to the opera. Once. I did not pay her 'very particular attentions.'"

"What actually occurred is beside the point. It's what people *say* that matters. And when you did not call again, how did that make Julia look? She spent two whole days locked in her bedchamber because she did not want to face anyone."

"If that is typical of Miss Thistlewaite's behavior, she has no cause to complain when people speak ill of her."

Cassie did not reply, letting his silence on the subject speak for itself. He assumed a wounded expression and, although Malcolm staunchly defended his friend whenever it was remarked that Lord Cassidy closely resembled a hound, Malcolm could not deny the likeness was particularly strong when Cassie was sulking.

"I *am* sorry, Cassie, that your cousin has become the target of gossips." The large brown eyes continued to stare at him reproachfully. "I did not set out to distress her, but neither am I going to propose marriage to a woman merely because I took her to the opera."

"No one said you had to," Cassie said.

"Perhaps not, but it is what they want. What are those dreams that I am accused of destroying? They are dreams of wedding the 'catch of the season' purely for the sake of my fortune and holdings. The only way I could fulfill the numerous expectations I have excited is to become a polygamist. If I even speak to a young lady, she is envisioning a trip down the aisle."

"So why not just choose some girl and make an end of it?" his friend asked.

"Why do you think I am here tonight? I am very anxious to find a suitable bride."

"What's wrong with Julia? She's generally acknowledged to be a handsome girl," Cassie said, though he couldn't quite meet his friend's eyes. Julia had harangued Cassie into discovering what she'd done to earn his friend's displeasure. Cassie was trying to do his cousinly duty by suggesting Julia as a suitable bride, but he felt uncomfortable doing so. He knew better than anyone just how annoying she could be.

"Your cousin is handsome enough," Malcolm agreed, "but she's not the girl for me."

"Why not?" Cassie asked.

"I don't know," Malcolm said, shrugging his shoulders. "She flutters her eyelashes too much."

"What? She flutters her eyelashes too much? *That* is the reason you did not call on her again?"

"It was very distracting. I thought a few times she was dozing off. Once I thought she was about to swoon, so I grabbed her arm. *That* made her eyes open quickly enough. I think she believed her quivering eyelashes had incited me to make her an offer of marriage."

Cassie just shook his head, those canine eyes of his expressing disappointment.

"Don't look at me like that, Cassie. That was not the only thing that decided me against Miss Thistlewaite." Malcolm reached into his waistcoat pocket and withdrew a piece of paper. He unfolded it while Cassie attempted to look at it over his shoulder. It appeared to Cassie to be a list of some kind. Malcolm perused it carefully while Cassie strained to see what it said. He saw "Possesses musical or artistic talent" and "Has genteel relations" before the paper was waved triumphantly in front of his face, Malcolm apparently having discovered what he was looking for.

"Here it is. Item four: 'Converses in a sensible fashion.' The only type of conversation Miss Thistlewaite enjoys is one composed entirely of flirtatious remarks or flowery compliments. When I asked her what opinion she held about the Corn Laws, she replied that restraint in one's diet was bound to have a healthful effect."

Cassie did not express any amusement upon hearing of his cousin's faux pas. He hurriedly changed the subject, as he did not want to become involved in a dull political discussion. "What is that, Malcolm? Is that a list?" Cassie tried to remove it from Malcolm's hand, but Malcolm hurriedly folded it and returned it to his waistcoat pocket.

"Yes, it is."

"You have some sort of list of qualifications for a bride?" Cassie asked, his voice higher than usual.

"So?"

"So, that is demmed arrogant of you, if you ask me. No wonder you cannot settle upon anyone. You want them to meet some catalog of requirements, like, like . . . a tandem horse you're purchasing from Tattersalls."

Malcolm seized upon his friend's analogy. "Exactly. I have definite requirements when filling my stable. Why should I not have even more stringent requirements for a bride? It is absolutely absurd to spend more time examining a horse than a wife, a lifelong companion you will see morning, noon, and night."

Since Cassie was of that breed of Englishman that considered a *horse* a lifelong companion to be seen morning, noon, and night, his friend's argument may not have carried the force it was meant to. He just muttered, "Next thing you know, you'll be putting her through her paces and checking her teeth."

Cassie avoided Julia for nearly a week after his conversation with Malcolm, but upon receiving her third missive, he presented himself at his aunt's town house. In her letter Julia had declared her intention of calling on him herself, unescorted, and he was well aware that his cousin was hotheaded enough to embroil them both in scandal if pushed too far.

He awaited Julia in the drawing room, looking about him in disapproval. Everything was in the first style of elegance, but his aunt seemed to have gone too far in following the Prince Regent's latest taste for chinoiserie. Every sofa or chair handle had a dragon's head, and one cabinet was filled to overflowing with pieces of pottery, glazed ceramic animals, and stone carvings. He was examining one objet d'art closely, a figurine of a lion with its mouth open wide in a snarling grin, when his cousin spoke in his ear.

"He does not bite, you know."

He started violently at the sound of her voice, and she laughed at the success of her surprise. "You have the manners of a Billingsgate fishwife," he told her, waiting for his cousin to sit before trying to fold his lanky body into one of the uncomfortable chairs.

"I would not know, as I do not keep the low society you do." She waved away his indignant rebuttal, saying, "Do not worry; I shan't tell anyone that you find a small piece of pottery so intimidating." Cassie began sputtering again, but Julia hurried to the point. "What did Mr. Malcolm say? You promised you would speak to him at Lord Wesleigh's ball and I have not heard from you since."

Cassie eyed his cousin in irritation, cursing the fates for making it necessary for him to claim kinship with such a selfish, spoiled girl. Neither of them had siblings and they were only a few years apart in age, so their parents had forced them into each other's company from child-hood on. Cassie's conciliatory, easygoing disposition was no match for Julia's more forceful nature, so from an early age he'd become accustomed to acceding to all but her most outrageous of demands. Julia had been an attractive child and had grown into a pretty young woman, with au-burn hair, light green eyes, and delicate features. Her air of innocent fragility still managed to deceive most people as to her true nature, but Cassie was not fooled. There was nothing fragile about his cousin's will.

"Well?" she asked, drumming her fingers impatiently upon a dragon's head.

"Yes, well, Malcolm agreed you are a handsome girl—"

"Did he?" Julia asked, an expression of pleased surprise on her face. "That is good news. I must say, I thought I had displeased him in some way. This is better news than I'd hoped for—"

"Wait," Cassie said, interrupting her exultations. "He is not at all interested in you."

7

Cassie had not meant to make such a blunt pronouncement and felt a twinge of guilt when his cousin's face fell. He could not bear to see any lady cry, and so hurried to stave off the tears he thought he saw gathering in her eyes. "He's got this list, you see, and you did not meet the fourth qualification. I would have failed it as well, as I have no interest in politics and have always found the Corn Laws particularly confusing. I mean, what difference does it make if they grow the corn in Berkshire or France?"

Julia didn't answer, but Cassie was pleased to see there didn't appear to be any danger of her crying any longer. In fact, she looked almost ferocious. "He has a list?" she asked, in a voice that was far too calm.

"Yes, well, I must say I did not care for the idea at first myself, but when he explained it to me, I could see his point. What if the girl has some odd kick in her gallop?"

Julia ignored this seeming non sequitur and tried to return to the point of the discussion. "I would like to know what is on this list, Cassie. Did you see it?"

"Yes, but it would do you no good. No good at all. Even if you'd passed the Corn Laws test, your eyelashes irritate him to no end."

"My *eyelashes*? Is the man deranged?"

"No, not at all. You just cannot fool him with those tricks you pull. He despises flirtatious games."

Julia rose from her seat to pace furiously about the room, muttering things like: "The unmitigated gall!" and "What conceit!" Cassie rose when his cousin did, but she waved him back into his seat, where he shifted nervously, suddenly aware that he had said far too much.

When Julia halted abruptly in her pacing and started smiling, Cassie became even more apprehensive. He had seen that expression on Julia's face more times than he cared to remember, and it always boded ill.

"I have an absolutely brilliant idea," she announced.

"Somehow I doubt it," he replied.

Selina Dalton, expecting nothing more interesting than a letter from her parents, was the surprised recipient of a letter of invitation from her old school friend Julia Thistlewaite.

She had hoped for just such an invitation when she had written to Julia four months previously, but when she'd never even had a reply to her letter, she had given it up as useless. Julia had always been a difficult sort of friend, liable to blow hot and cold, so it had not surprised Selina too much when Julia refused to acknowledge their previous acquaintance. She was more amazed that Julia had finally invited Selina to stay with her at the Thistlewaites' town house in Berkeley Square.

Selina let out a small squeal of delight at the prospect before looking around guiltily. But, of course, there was no one to hear her. She was alone, as was usual, in the drawing room of her former mistress's home in Bath.

Mrs. Ossory had been a kind and benevolent mistress,

and Selina had been genuinely grieved upon her death four months previously. They had lived harmoniously together for three years after Selina took up her position as companion. Her duties were not at all onerous, and Mrs. Ossory had proved as much a companion to Selina as Selina had to her. Even in death she had been generous, leaving Selina a small settlement.

However, Selina could not go on living indefinitely in Mrs. Ossory's town house, which had been bequeathed to a nephew. And she did not really want to return to the small parish in Sussex where her father was serving as vicar. She had hoped when she had accepted the post with Mrs. Ossory that she might eventually contract an engagement to a suitable gentleman while living in Bath. Her parents did not have the money to expend on a London season, but when Mrs. Ossory, a distant connection of her mother's, mentioned that she was looking for a companion, Selina had leapt at the opportunity. Here was her chance to experience life outside the vicarage. And perhaps, if she made a suitable match, to be in a position to sponsor her younger brothers and sisters.

Selina had enjoyed her time in Bath and had not regretted the three years she'd spent there, but she had felt that there was something missing. Mrs. Ossory's circle of friends and acquaintances had, by necessity, become Selina's acquaintances, and there was not anyone under fifty among them. She felt the lack of society of those of her own age and interests, and felt that perhaps she could find such society in London.

But she realized a young lady of two-and-twenty could not live alone, so she had written Julia, who Selina knew could give her entrée to the society she sought. And, lo and behold, she had finally received the prized invitation.

It arrived just after Selina had made the decision to return home to her family, realizing that she had delayed the inevitable long enough. She'd made arrangements to leave Bath the following morning and was grateful the letter had not arrived one day later, because now her destination was London.

Selina was a little taken aback by her reception when she arrived in London two days later. Julia waved away Selina's apologies for arriving so soon, interrupting Selina in the middle of her explanation by saying, "It is better this way. We can begin immediately." She then proceeded to circle Selina as she stood in the drawing room, eyeing her critically.

"I suppose we will have to make do," she finally said, and Selina felt the urge to apologize for her inadequacies although she still had no idea what Julia was talking about.

Realizing that some response was called for, Selina said, "I beg your pardon?"

Julia, startled out of her ruminations, gave a tinkling laugh and apologized for her odd behavior. "I will explain all to you shortly, but I am waiting for my cousin Lord Cassidy to arrive."

Selina nodded, though still at a loss, and Julia began chattering excitedly. "Please come and sit down so we can renew our acquaintance. Tell me, what have you been doing this—has it really been five years?"

Selina assured her that it had been five years since they had last seen each other, and explained about her tenure as Mrs. Ossory's companion.

"How very dreary for you," Julia said.

"It was not at all unpleasant, though I did long for some companions my own age. Bath has become quite the destination for septuagenarians seeking the fountain of youth."

"I completely understand. I find foreigners extremely tedious as well." Before Selina could explain to Julia she had actually misunderstood, Julia continued: "And I am sure you found little in the way of entertainment. You will be treated much better here in London."

Selina, beginning to remember how selfish Julia used to be, rather doubted the truth of her statement, but felt it rude to contradict her hostess. She was then regaled with a recital of the delights that awaited her, but as Julia's conversation mostly consisted of the names of people Selina was destined to meet but that currently held no meaning for her, she was hard-pressed to appear interested. So she was quite relieved when Lord Cassidy finally arrived.

Julia made the introductions and Selina eyed Lord Cassidy with interest, thinking that she had not been in London for two hours and had already made the acquaintance of a young gentleman. The interest eventually faded to amusement, however, as she decided that Cassie, as he insisted upon being called, could have been torn from one of Cruikshank's cartoons.

His features, while pleasant, seemed somewhat exaggerated, so that his eyes, ears, and nose all appeared slightly too big for his face. His arms and legs were long and skinny; his clothing, while fashionable and expensive, was creased and rumpled. And though he smiled genially at Selina, his expressive face took on a scowl whenever he glanced in the direction of his cousin Julia.

"So, now that my cousin is here, I thought I would explain to you the reason I invited you to London," Julia said, once everyone was seated. Sensing Selina's surprise at this statement, as Julia had said in her letter she'd issued the invitation because she wished the pleasure of Selina's company, she hurried to explain. "Of course, you know I've always enjoyed your company, dear Selina, which was the reason I even conceived of inviting you, but I also felt that while you were residing in town you might undertake to help me with a little project."

"A project?" Selina prompted, as Julia hesitated at that point and seemed loath to go on.

Julia glanced at her cousin, who only scowled more ferociously at her. Julia continued undaunted, although she appeared to be having difficulty meeting Selina's gaze. "Perhaps 'project' is not the right word," she said. "It's really more of a lark."

"Humph," Cassie snorted, and rolled his eyes.

His cousin ignored him and said, "You see, there is a young gentleman, a Mr. Malcolm, who is widely known for his arrogance. He distinguished me by paying me very pointed attentions, but then humiliated me by withdrawing his suit."

"How dreadful for you! I am so sorry."

Julia waved away Selina's expressions of sympathy with an impatient gesture. "Yes, it was quite unpleasant, particularly when I discovered that he has a list that he judged me against, and found me wanting."

"He has a list? What sort of list?"

"It is a list of the qualifications he is looking for in a bride. But he believes himself to be so superior to the rest of us that the qualifications are quite unreachable. I would love to see Mr. Malcolm receive the comeuppance he deserves by playing a small prank on him. And I remembered how in school you were up for any sort of lark." Selina was given no opportunity to object to this reading of her character—though Selina herself remembered nothing of the sort—as Julia continued, "I thought if we were to present you as the perfect woman he is looking for, and then allow him to discover *you* have a list, and he does not meet the qualifications on *your* list, it would be a perfect sort of poetic justice."

"But, Julia, if he is as arrogant and fastidious as you say, surely I will not attract his attention, either?"

"There is that possibility, but then, you are better informed than I or any other young lady has been. You know about the list, and with some tutelage from me and my cousin, you have a much better chance of meeting the requirements."

Selina glanced over at Lord Cassidy, wondering how this disheveled, comical-looking man could tutor her in the feminine wiles necessary to attract a refined gentleman of particular tastes. He saw her wondering glance and explained: "Malcolm's my good friend. I know him better than most."

"And you agree he deserves this prank played on him?" Selina asked.

Julia replied before Cassie could. "Of course he does. He would not have offered his assistance if he did not think so." When Selina continued to protest, Julia said impatiently, "Do not be such a namby-pamby, Selina. You will not be doing anything to Mr. Malcolm that he has not already done himself to more than one young lady, myself included."

"It is just that I think your little prank is doomed to failure. If Mr. Malcolm was not captivated by you, Julia, I doubt he will even look in my direction."

Cassie wondered what his cousin would say to that. He knew she hated to play second fiddle to any woman, but there was no denying that his cousin paled in comparison to Selina. Where Julia's hair was light red, Selina's was a dark, rich reddish-brown. Where Julia's eyes were pale green, Selina's were a lustrous emerald green. Where Julia's complexion was a fashionable white, Selina's skin had a golden cast, almost as if she were glowing. Any gentleman would look in Selina's direction and, once they had, they would continue looking.

Julia mentioned none of that, however. "While it's true you are not a beauty in the *classical* sense, I think in the right setting and with the correct set of circumstances, you can attract Mr. Malcolm's attention," she said.

Selina shook her head, saying, "I don't think—"

"I must say," Julia interrupted her, "this little prank is the only thing that has tempted me to venture back into society. I do hope you'll agree to help me, or we may have to cut your delightful visit short. I doubt I would be in the mood for socializing."

Selina immediately grasped Julia's meaning. She had been invited with a specific purpose, that of assisting Julia in humbling Mr. Malcolm. If she refused to help Julia in this endeavor, any entrée into London society would be denied her. She sighed, weighing her options. As much as she disliked the idea, it did sound as if Mr. Malcolm would be receiving his just deserts. And there was always the very real probability he would never even notice her, in which case Julia could not blame her if the plan failed.

"What is it you want me to do?" Selina asked, and Julia smiled in triumph.

2

One week later, Selina was regretting her hasty agreement to Julia's plan. She had already spent most of
her annual income on the new wardrobe that Julia said
was essential to catching Mr. Malcolm's eye, she had yet
to attend even the most innocuous social event, and her
head was spinning with the contradictory instructions
Julia was giving her.

"You must exude a certain elegance of mind, a knowledge of the world, while still retaining the naïveté that
gentlemen find so charming," she told Selina as they sat
beside each other on a sofa in the Thistlewaites' drawing
room, with Cassie sitting across from them.

"Do you know anything about the Corn Laws?" Cassie
asked Selina.

"Yes, of course."

"It's very important that you do. I've brought you some tracts on the subject," Cassie said.

"Don't waste too much time on those tracts, Selina. A gentleman doesn't like a lady to be more intelligent than him. Isn't that right, Cassie?" Julia smiled mischievously at her cousin, who scowled at her. "And thinking too intensely causes forehead furrows." Julia gently touched the area between Selina's brows. "It might be a good idea if you were to meditate on the ocean. I have found if I think of the sea, I'm less apt to wrinkle my brow."

"Oh, I almost forgot," Cassie said. "No winking."

"I beg your pardon?" Selina said.

"Malcolm doesn't like flirtatious tricks."

"Cassie, if you were paying the least bit of attention, you would have realized that I already said that. I explained to Selina that there should be no artificiality in her behavior when she pretends an attraction to Mr. Malcolm."

"That doesn't sound anything at all like what I said," Cassie said.

"Pardon me for not using words of fewer syllables—"

"Well if you are so smart, Miss Hoity-Toity, why couldn't you pass Malcolm's little test?"

"Perhaps if you'd warned me—"

Selina had heard enough. "Stop it this instant!" she said, breaking into their argument. The cousins turned to look at her, their eyes big. "I have heard enough of your bickering this week to last me a lifetime. I believe I have an idea of what Mr. Malcolm is looking for. Now, what plan do you have for us to meet?"

Selina, peeking out from behind the door of her host's library, could not believe this was the manner in which she was spending her first ball. She had been introduced to her hostess, Mrs. Harrington, danced one dance with Cassie, and then ushered into the library to hide for the rest of the evening. Mr. Malcolm was apparently in attendance and her cohorts felt that she should present an air of mystery to pique his interest. After her first dance she was to disappear while Julia and Cassie mingled with the rest of those in attendance, whispering about the new Incognita.

Selina could not help but reflect that the society in Bath, as elderly as it was, was superior to that of the harebrained cousins. "I should have gone to Sussex after all," she said aloud, still standing at the door and peering into the empty hallway.

"I beg your pardon?" a voice said from behind her.

She whirled around to see a young man standing in the room, apparently having risen from his seat at her entrance. And the sight of him made her very glad she had not gone to Sussex. He was the most beautiful man she had ever seen. The library was not well lit—evidently the Harringtons did not expect their guests to seek refuge there in the middle of a ball—so Selina could only hope that when seen in the full light of day, he would look less like a Greek god and more like a mere mortal.

"I am sorry to disturb you, sir," Selina said when she finally recovered from her surprise.

"It is no matter," he said, folding a paper he held in his hand and slipping it into his pocket. "I was just reflecting on the futility of a dream."

Selina, who had been reflecting likewise just moments ago, was now thinking that perhaps she'd been overly hasty. "Is any dream futile? It gives us hope, and hope is a good thing."

"In your opinion. Others of us may believe, as the poet said, 'Hope is the most hopeless thing of all.'"

"What a sad conviction to hold! I prefer to believe, like Johnson, that hope is the 'chief happiness which this world affords.' But perhaps you hope for something unworthy, in which case you deserve to hope in vain. Confess, sir, you were hoping to win at the gaming tables and you have lost, and now you are indulging in a fit of pique."

The mysterious gentleman smiled. "I would not confess to such childish conduct, although had I played, I would have hoped to win."

"So you contend that you hope for something worthy."

"I do indeed."

"Then it is my hope that you obtain it," Selina said, smiling.

"I am honored. Perhaps I am mistaken in thinking hope a useless thing," he said, staring intently at Selina.

Her smile faltered a little and there was an awkward silence. Selina was suddenly aware that she should not have remained alone in the library with a strange gentleman carrying on a philosophical discussion. "I am sorry I disturbed you. I should go," she finally said, but made no move to leave. She realized as soon as the words left her mouth that she had nowhere *to* go. She had been instructed by Cassie and Julia to stay where she was until they returned for her. Thankfully, the gentleman said he should be the one to leave, and walked to the door, where she still stood.

She stepped aside but he paused in front of her. "I would be delighted if you would save a dance for me, once you return to the ballroom and we have been properly introduced."

Selina just nodded, suddenly shy. It was only after he left the room that she remembered she would not be returning to the ballroom.

Mr. Malcolm entered the ballroom to find his friend Cassie searching for him.

"Where have you been? I've got a likely prospect for you. Young filly, deep-chested, long legs . . ."

Malcolm was regretting having ever used that horse analogy. Cassie had described every young lady he'd seen since in equine terms.

"I am not interested, Cassie. I think I've found a likely prospect of my own."

"What? You couldn't have!" Cassie exclaimed. Malcolm looked at him in surprise.

"I thought you wanted me to find a suitable young lady."

"I do, I do. It's just that there's a new girl in town everyone's talking about. She's visiting my cousin Julia for a few weeks. She has quite the air of mystery about her."

"That sounds rather alarming. I tend to keep my distance from mysterious young ladies. It usually turns out they're pining away for their dancing master or someone equally unsuitable."

"No such thing, I assure you," Cassie said, but Malcolm ignored him, casually surveying the ballroom.

"I wonder how long she will be in the library," Malcolm muttered, and Cassie looked up, startled.

"What's that?" he asked his friend.

"Oh, nothing of consequence," Malcolm said. "She'll probably turn out to be married or equally ineligible," he mumbled to himself.

Cassie looked searchingly at his friend for a moment before excusing himself. Malcolm just nodded, still scanning the ballroom for the lady from the library, though he found himself ambivalent about meeting her a second time. He had been quite impressed with her, but was worried that when he encountered her again, he'd find that he'd endowed her with nonexistent qualities in his eagerness to find an eligible bride. She had seemed like an answer to a prayer, arriving in the library so suddenly when he had almost convinced himself his quest was futile. Even in the darkness of the library she'd sparkled. Her large eyes glowed with intelligence and humor, and her smile enchanted him with its sweet sincerity. The more he thought about her, the more his ambivalence faded and he became impatient to see her again, so he could discover for himself the exact color of those fascinating eyes.

Cassie rushed to the library to find Selina sitting disconsolately on a sofa, staring into space.

"Miss Dalton, did you meet a gentleman in here?" he asked.

Selina looked up, startled by Cassie's sudden entrance. "What? Oh, yes. Yes, I did. He was beautiful. He asked me to dance." The thought of missing that dance caused Selina to frown. She wondered what there was for Cassie to grin about.

"Excellent," he said. "I think we should return to the ballroom so that you can have that dance."

"Really? Do you know the gentleman?" Selina asked.

"I rather think I do," Cassie replied, smiling even more broadly.

Cassie and Selina joined Mrs. Thistlewaite, who was awaiting Julia's return from her dance. Mrs. Thistlewaite was a petite, timid woman with "delicate nerves." She was no match for her headstrong daughter and allowed Julia an inordinate amount of independence. She and her husband had been approaching middle age when Julia was born, so Julia's birth was greeted as a miracle. Mr. Thistlewaite had been an indulgent father during his lifetime, and even now Julia was able to coerce her mother on those few occasions she opposed Julia by saying: "Papa would have allowed it."

Mrs. Thistlewaite greeted her nephew and Selina warmly, rising at their approach and dropping her shawl on the floor. Selina recovered it for her.

"Oh, how clumsy of me. Thank you, Selina. Such a dear girl. But why have you not been dancing? I have not seen you dance with anyone other than Cassie."

Selina and Cassie exchanged a look, but Julia arrived just at that moment and thankfully a reply was not necessary.

"Cassie! What is Selina doing here? You are going to ruin all of my efforts. Everyone is fascinated by the new Incognita. If they actually see Selina, they will no longer be interested in her."

"Why, thank you, Julia," Selina said.

Cassie began to tell Julia about the meeting in the library when he was interrupted by the arrival of Mr. Malcolm.

Selina, still unaware of the identity of the mysterious man from the library, was thrilled to see him again. In the brighter light of the ballroom she was able to determine he was just as handsome as he had first appeared. This had the unfortunate effect of making it difficult for her to breathe, or to think. So it took a few moments for her to realize how her mysterious stranger was being addressed by Cassie.

"Mr. *Malcolm*!" Selina said in surprise, and then flushed when all heads swiveled in her direction.

Malcolm, his eyebrows raised, smiled quizzically at Selina. "That is correct. I, however, have not yet learned your name." He then turned to his friend Cassie to perform the honors.

"Mr. Malcolm, may I present Miss Dalton."

"Miss Dalton, I am pleased to make your acquaintance," Mr. Malcolm said, bowing over her hand.

Selina sank into a curtsy and hoped desperately she would be able to rise again, for her legs suddenly seemed too weak to support her. *This* was the insufferably arrogant man who went around breaking ladies' hearts? The ridiculous charade she was embarking on now seemed more impossible than ever. Selina knew she was no more immune to a glance from those dark eyes than any other woman. If Julia, who was much more sophisticated than Selina, had succumbed, what chance did she, a lowly vicar's daughter, have against those seductive, glittering orbs and that devastating smile?

Mr. Malcolm requested the next dance, but before Selina could collect her scattered wits to make a reply, Julia had stepped between them and addressed him.

"Unfortunately, sir, you have arrived too late. Miss Dalton has been besieged by admirers since she arrived and has promised all of her dances. Regrettably, I have not enjoyed such success and have this dance free."

Mr. Malcolm hid his disappointment remarkably well. "Then perhaps I could have the honor of this dance?" he asked Julia.

Julia accepted with a commanding glare at her cousin Cassie, who offered his arm to Selina. Apparently he was to dance with Selina once again to give credence to Julia's lie. Selina wondered where the rest of her partners were to come from, but when she exited the dance floor, she was surrounded by eager gentlemen and danced every dance for what was left of the evening. Unfortunately, every gentleman she met paled in comparison to Mr. Malcolm, who left the ball shortly after his dance with Julia.

3

As Julia and Selina sat with Mrs. Thistlewaite in the drawing room awaiting the morning's callers, Julia explained to Selina that there would probably not be as many as usual, as the London season had officially ended a few weeks ago. Julia had a great many other things to say as well, but Selina, although pretending to listen, was instead wondering how to act should Mr. Malcolm call.

"Selina, are you listening to me?" Julia finally asked in a sharp tone of voice.

"Why, of course, Julia. You were lectur—that is, you were advising me."

"So you agree with what I said?"

"Of course I do. You have the greater experience in these matters," Selina said absently, thinking that perhaps she should have worn a more demure gown. Her salmon-colored gown was very stylish, but she thought it might be a little too flashy in combination with her hair. But Julia, who was a pattern card of elegance, had assured her it was "just the thing," so she comforted herself with that knowledge.

The butler announced the first caller, a Lord Sylvester Mountjoy, and Selina shook off her abstraction to entertain Lord Sylvester, one of her dance partners from the previous evening. Fairly soon the Thistlewaites' drawing room was filled with eager young gentlemen, and Selina found herself enjoying her social success and almost forgetting Mr. Malcolm. So she was quite startled when Reeves, the Thistlewaites' butler, announced him.

Mr. Malcolm strode into the room, greeting Mrs. Thistlewaite and Julia before approaching Selina.

"Good day, Miss Dalton. I trust I find you in good health?"

"Yes indeed, sir," Selina stammered, feeling suddenly gauche and unsophisticated. "And you?"

"I am quite well, thank you."

There was an uncomfortable pause as Mr. Malcolm stood in front of Selina and Selina's admirers eyed him jealously. All the seats near Selina were taken, and it was obvious none of the young gentlemen would willingly surrender his seat to Mr. Malcolm.

"I hate to remove you from such pleasant company, Miss Dalton, but I am forced to remind you of our appointment."

"Our appointment?" Selina repeated, at a loss. She was further bewildered when one of Mr. Malcolm's eyes quickly closed and reopened in a wink.

"Surely you cannot have forgotten? You promised me the previous evening that you would drive with me today, when I was not fortunate enough to secure a dance with you."

Selina could not help but be flattered at Mr. Malcolm's obvious ploy to remove her from the midst of her admirers. She shared a secret smile with him but, before she could reply, Julia once again intervened.

"Selina, do not forget that you agreed to drive with Cassie this afternoon. He will be arriving at any moment."

"I am sure Cassie will not mind if Miss Dalton drives out with me. He had the privilege of dancing with her last night, whereas I was not similarly honored," Mr. Malcolm said.

"But when I asked Selina this morning if she was looking forward to her drive with Cassie, she *agreed* that it was a good idea," Julia said, her voice full of meaning.

Selina realized that she must have unwittingly agreed to pretend to be otherwise occupied if Mr. Malcolm invited her out. She understood Julia's strategy in wanting her to appear to be unattainable, but she felt that Julia was in danger of going too far.

"I am sorry, Julia. I'd forgotten I'd agreed to drive with Mr. Malcolm already," Selina said.

"Miss Dalton appears to be a very *agreeable* young lady," Lord Sylvester said in his high-pitched voice. A few of the gentlemen dutifully laughed at his little quip.

"That is certainly one way to describe her," Julia said, glaring at Selina from across the room.

"Miss Thistlewaite," Malcolm said with an impatient glance in Julia's direction, "while I appreciate your loyalty to your cousin, I am sure Cassie will not mind if I take Miss Dalton for a drive."

"I will collect my things," Selina said, jumping up from her seat before Julia could devise some other stratagem to keep her and Mr. Malcolm apart.

Selina ran up the stairs to her chamber and quickly put on her hat and spencer, which had a standing lace collar and looked quite dashing in combination with her dress. She found she wanted to look her best for Mr. Malcolm, for reasons that had nothing whatsoever to do with Julia's little scheme.

Descending the stairs, she saw Mr. Malcolm waiting for her, silhouetted by the light streaming in from the fanlight above the door, and she thought once again how unfair it was for a man to be so handsome.

"I am ready," she said, stopping in front of him.

"Not quite," he said, and moved forward until there was not even six inches between them. Selina held her breath as his hands came toward her face and grasped her hat, tilting it a little to one side. "Now you are ready," he said.

"Thank you," she whispered.

"My pleasure," he said, and smiled. Selina thought he was entirely too close; his nearness was having an unusual effect on her. However, Mr. Malcolm seemed undisturbed, merely giving Selina his arm and leading her down the steps of the town house and toward his curricle.

Selina was still not accustomed to riding in such a dainty, high-perched vehicle. The only other time she had ridden in a curricle was with Cassie, and he became distracted far too easily to inspire confidence. But Mr. Malcolm appeared to be very much in control, and soon Selina relaxed and began to enjoy herself.

"Miss Thistlewaite appears determined to keep us from enjoying each other's company," Mr. Malcolm said to Selina, having safely negotiated them through some London traffic.

"I beg your pardon?" Selina said, turning to look at him. But his expression gave nothing away.

"Your friend Miss Thistlewaite. She appears to be manufacturing excuses to keep us apart."

"Really? I had not noticed," Selina said, fidgeting nervously with her glove to avoid meeting Mr. Malcolm's sideways glance.

"You had to have noticed. It was obvious to the meanest intelligence. Miss Thistlewaite was not exactly subtle."

Selina realized she could no longer evade the topic by

pretending to be ignorant of Julia's behavior. "Perhaps Julia is merely looking out for my best interests," she said.

"How so?"

"Well, you have a certain reputation as a—" Selina hesitated, searching for the correct, least offensive word.

"Trifler?" Mr. Malcolm suggested.

"Well, yes."

"A Breaker of Hearts?"

"I suppose one could say that."

"A Destroyer of Young Ladies' Dreams?" Malcolm recited.

"That's an absurd exaggeration, but I have heard rumors along those lines."

"And you believe this description of me?" Malcolm asked Selina.

Selina hesitated, looking over at Mr. Malcolm. He looked as handsome and urbane as ever, but his expression was severe, as if he was strictly controlling his countenance. While Selina was watching him, he glanced over at her, and she was struck by how vulnerable he suddenly appeared.

"I am not certain *what* to believe," she told him, and was rewarded by his smiling at her.

"I am relieved to hear you say that, Miss Dalton, because I do not feel I deserve the reputation I have acquired. Particularly in Miss Thistlewaite's case do I feel myself blameless."

"She told me that you paid her very marked attentions."

"I escorted her to the opera."

"You escorted her to the opera," Selina repeated.

"Once."

"Was it an amusing opera?" Selina asked, suddenly struck by the absurdity of the situation.

Mr. Malcolm considered the question. "No, it was not an amusing opera. The soprano missed most of her notes, and Miss Thistlewaite wore a feather in her hair."

"A feather?"

"It brushed my nose frequently that evening and I found myself wanting to sneeze," Malcolm said, maintaining a serious countenance. It was only when he glanced Selina's way that she saw the glint of humor in his eyes.

"I completely understand," Selina said.

"Do you?" Malcolm asked.

"I do indeed. You and Miss Thistlewaite are the victims of a most egregious set of circumstances. Feathers and screeching sopranos are not conducive to romance. Even the greatest and most historic pair of lovers would be daunted by circumstances such as those," Selina said with mock gravity.

"So you acquit me of trifling with Miss Thistlewaite's affections?"

"I am afraid I cannot. You were too easily put off, you see. A sincere gentleman would have tried again. Invited her to a musical concert, perhaps."

"But I knew I was not interested in Miss Thistlewaite after the opera. If I had continued to pursue her, I would have deserved the reputation I've acquired."

"Perhaps you are right," Selina said. "Poor Julia. I can understand her disappointment. It must be quite humiliating to inspire no stronger inclination in a gentleman than that to sneeze."

"Oh, I did not say that. Miss Thistlewaite has inspired other longings in me from time to time."

"Really?" Selina asked, feeling that the conversation, which had been such fun only moments before, had suddenly gone awry.

"Oh, yes. For instance, just this afternoon I longed quite fervently to stuff my cravat in her mouth."

Selina laughed a little harder than the joke perhaps called for, so relieved was she that Mr. Malcolm's longings were not of the amorous sort. "Please, let us not speak of Julia anymore. I am feeling traitorous."

"I am more than happy to comply. Let us discuss you instead."

"Me?" Selina asked, surprised.

"Yes. Please tell me about yourself."

"You must be aware that there is no more effective way to stifle conversation than to request that someone talk about oneself. None of us would willingly discuss our faults, and were we to discuss our strengths we would be termed a braggart, and rightly so."

"I suppose you are correct. You must forgive me, but in my limited experience with the gentler sex they always seem more than willing to discuss themselves," Mr. Malcolm said wryly, and Selina gathered from his tone that his limited experience with her sex was not necessarily a pleasant one. She could not quite bring herself to believe that a gentleman as good-looking as he was could have only a *limited* experience of her sex. But perhaps his fastidiousness had kept him insulated from too much interaction with women. She found herself hoping so. The thought of him involved in numerous *affaires* greatly displeased her for some reason.

Before she could reply, their conversation was interrupted by a man's voice shouting, "Jeremy Malcolm?"

Malcolm and Selina had been circling Hyde Park, but as it was not yet the fashionable hour of five o'clock, there were not too many others engaged in a similar pastime. The few inhabitants of the park seemed to consist mostly of nannies and their charges and a few lone horsemen. One of those horsemen had approached them and was addressing Malcolm.

Mr. Malcolm reined in, at first appearing displeased at the interruption but then regarding the interloper with delight. "Henry, old man, this is a surprise! I thought you were stationed with your regiment in the north."

"Yes, well, I decided to sell out and join the ranks of you idle gentlemen wastrels."

"Are you sure you're prepared for it? It can be quite exhausting," Malcolm said, grinning at his friend. He then remembered his lady companion and, turning to her, said, "Miss Dalton, may I present Mr. Henry Ossory?"

"Miss Dalton?" Mr. Ossory said at the same time Selina was saying, "Mr. Ossory?"

The handsome, fair-haired young gentleman wearing a black armband looked at first surprised and then delighted. "Miss Selina Dalton?" he asked, smiling at her.

Malcolm eyed them a little jealously. "I take it you two are familiar with each other?"

"Miss Dalton was an excellent friend to my uncle's widow. I am actually here in London because I wanted to thank her for her kindness to my aunt."

"I am very pleased to meet you, sir," Selina told him. "I esteemed your aunt very highly and have long wished to express my condolences to you."

"Thank you," Mr. Ossory said, his bright smile fading for a moment. "I am sorry I did not get to see her once more before she died."

Mr. Ossory's horse whinnied and he reached down to pat it. "I should probably let you resume your drive, but I would be pleased to call on you, Miss Dalton, if you would give me your direction."

"I am staying at the Thistlewaites' town house in Berkeley Square," she told him, giving him the number. "I would be pleased to receive you."

"Thank you. I will call on you shortly. Good day, Miss

Dalton. Malcolm." Mr. Ossory rode away, leaving Mr. Malcolm and Selina alone together once again.

"What a fortuitous meeting," Selina said as she watched Mr. Ossory ride away.

"Quite," Mr. Malcolm rejoined rather grimly.

4

$\mathcal{S}$elina returned from her drive to find a seething Julia waiting for her. She had barely entered the house before Julia pounced on her and pulled her into the now empty drawing room.

"Selina! Why did you drive out with Mr. Malcolm? We agreed it would be better for you to avoid being alone with him for a few days longer to ensure you captured his interest."

"I am sorry, Julia, but it seemed the thing to do. Besides, I am not so sure this idea of yours is a good one. I like Mr. Malcolm. He does not seem arrogant to me."

"You are naïve. I *told* you that he trifled with me and humiliated me."

"But he told me that he merely escorted you to the opera. That does not seem such a heinous crime."

"Did he mention the list? Did he tell you about my eyelashes?" Julia said, growing agitated.

"What?" Selina asked.

"He is so critical, so judgmental. Nothing pleases the man. Just wait until he starts weighing you against that list of his. Then you'll discover how very unpleasant he can be."

"Please calm down, Julia. You are overwrought," Selina said, becoming seriously alarmed. Julia sounded quite hysterical.

"Selina, please say you'll help me. There is nothing I can do to touch him; he holds all of London society in his palm. This is the only way, don't you see?" Julia had grasped Selina's shoulders, and Selina was dismayed to see that she looked as if she was about to cry.

"I just do not think he is the villain you paint him, Julia. Perhaps you should spend more time with him, get to know him better."

Julia stomped her foot like a child having a tantrum. "I do not wish to know him any better! I want him humiliated, as I was."

"I think you are overreacting to the situation," Selina said, convinced now that her old school friend suffered from nothing more than wounded pride. There was a long pause while Julia regained her composure and drew herself up haughtily.

"And I think that I made a mistake inviting you here. Perhaps you had better return to Bath."

Selina stared at Julia, surprised that she could be so vindictive. "Perhaps you are right," she told her, and turned around to leave the room.

Julia ran to block the door, preventing Selina from leaving. "Please, Selina, I was not serious about you returning to Bath. Please stay."

Selina continued to stare at Julia coldly. "I do not think I would like to stay under these circumstances."

"I understand," Julia said. A tear ran unheeded down her cheek. "Everyone takes his side," she said sadly.

"I am not taking any side—"

"It is all right," Julia said, smiling bravely. "I have known you for years and you have known Mr. Malcolm less than one day, but I realize I cannot compete with him. He has this effect on all women. He exercises some kind of power over them."

"He did not exercise any power . . ." Selina started to say, and then faltered. Could Julia be right? Selina felt more strongly attracted to Mr. Malcolm than any other man she had ever met. Whenever his hand swept against hers, whenever he smiled at her with that perfect mouth and those even white teeth, whenever he stared at her from those dark brown eyes, she was shaken to the core of her being.

Julia watched Selina, a knowing smile on her face. "I am just asking you to think on it, Selina. Just think on it."

"All right, Julia. I will."

"Good," Julia said, clapping her hands together in glee. Selina could only marvel at the mercurial moods of her friend and hope she would not have occasion to witness such extremes again.

Selina spent a restless night thinking it over, and was unable to reach a satisfying conclusion. Was Mr. Malcolm a scoundrel who made a career of breaking women's hearts, or was Julia merely a spoiled brat out for revenge? It was difficult to know, and Selina finally realized the only way to determine the truth was to spend more time in Mr. Malcolm's company. Since this was what she wanted to do anyway, it was not hard for her to convince herself this was the best course of action. But she resolved to guard her heart as she did so. She did not want to be the latest in his string of conquests.

After breakfast, she and the Thistlewaites awaited the morning callers in the drawing room. Selina hoped Mr. Malcolm would call and could barely contain her excitement at the prospect. When Reeves announced to the ladies that they had a caller, she was sure it was him.

"Who is it, Reeves?" asked Mrs. Thistlewaite.

"A Mr. Ossory, madam."

"I am not acquainted with a Mr. Ossory," Mrs. Thistlewaite said, looking bewildered.

Selina had nearly forgotten her meeting with Mr. Ossory the day before, but although she was a little disappointed he was not Mr. Malcolm, she was pleased at the opportunity to further her acquaintance with a young gentleman Mrs. Ossory had always spoken of very favorably. "It's all right, Mrs. Thistlewaite," Selina told her. "He is an acquaintance of mine. I should like to see him."

"Certainly, dear. Show him in, Reeves."

Selina greeted Mr. Ossory before introducing him to Julia and Mrs. Thistlewaite, who expressed their pleasure in meeting him. Selina was struck anew by the handsome appearance he presented and, if she hadn't already made Mr. Malcolm's acquaintance, felt she may have been in danger of falling victim to Mr. Ossory's boyish good looks and open countenance.

He spent the requisite fifteen minutes in conversation with the three ladies before requesting the honor of a drive with Selina.

Selina acquiesced and found herself helped into yet another sporting vehicle and once again led off in the direction of Hyde Park.

"I am not sure if you are aware of the fact that my aunt mentioned you many times in her correspondence with me, Miss Dalton," Mr. Ossory said.

"No, I was not aware of it. I am not surprised, however. Your aunt never once treated me as someone in service, but always as a beloved friend and a—a *companion* in the truest sense of the word."

"I know she was quite fond of your mother and looked

upon you as she would a granddaughter. Which is the reason I sought you out. I did so at her request."

"How kind of you. I must confess I was somewhat curious about you as well. Your aunt spoke of you quite often. I'm very pleased to have this opportunity to make your acquaintance."

"I feel likewise. However, I must admit to yet another motive in seeking you out."

Mr. Ossory paused and seemed loath to continue.

"Yes?" Selina prompted him.

"I came to town to meet you because it is my belief that my aunt desired us to make a match."

Selina could feel her heart begin to beat uncomfortably fast. "What"—she paused to clear her throat before continuing a little more calmly—"what gave you that impression?"

"Her letter to me before her death. In it she wrote: 'It is my desire that you and Selina make a match.'"

"Oh. I see. Then it appears you interpreted her meaning correctly."

Selina found herself too shy to meet Mr. Ossory's gaze. There was an awkward silence between them until Selina peeked over at Mr. Ossory, who was at that moment looking at her. Their eyes met and suddenly Selina found herself giggling. Mr. Ossory began laughing as well.

"Yes, her words were rather plain. Unless of course she was speaking of cribbage. She could have meant that we should engage in a cribbage match."

Selina struggled to regain her composure. "Or chess! Could she not have been speaking of chess?"

Mr. Ossory shook his head solemnly. "I am afraid not. My aunt knew me to be a very poor chess player."

They were still laughing, while managing to offer suggestions for various matches such as "Cricket" and "Vingt-et-un," when they were interrupted by the approach of Mr. Malcolm. Mr. Malcolm found himself in the unenviable position of having to repeat his greeting twice before his friends noticed his presence.

"Good day, Henry, Miss Dalton," he said a second time, walking his horse beside the slowly moving curricle.

They finally looked up and Mr. Ossory brought his team to a halt. "Malcolm!" Mr. Ossory said, his open countenance radiating good humor. "How nice to see you."

"Good day, Mr. Malcolm," Selina said pleasantly.

"It appears I have interrupted a humorous discussion."

"Oh, it was nothing of consequence. We were merely discussing a letter Mr. Ossory received from his aunt," Selina said. Mr. Malcolm, never having met Mrs. Ossory, had no comment to make on that subject. The three fell into an uncomfortable silence.

"I wondered if you were to attend Lady Hartley's ball this evening," Malcolm finally said.

"I believe I am," Selina said.

"Excellent. Perhaps you can save me the first waltz and the supper dance."

"I would be pleased to."

Selina, realizing that they were excluding Mr. Ossory from the conversation, turned to speak to him. "And you, Mr. Ossory, do you attend Lady Hartley's ball this evening?"

"Unfortunately, no. I am unacquainted with Lady Hartley."

Malcolm could barely suppress a triumphant grin. He was very pleased to be getting Selina away from his so-called friend for the evening. Then he chanced to look at Selina, who was staring at him with a beseeching expression on her lovely face.

"Perhaps I could arrange an introduction," he heard himself say, and was rewarded by a bright smile from Selina. He was less pleased by the grin on Henry's face, although he managed a polite response to Henry's effusive expression of thanks.

"I shall see you both this evening," Malcolm said, and rode away.

Selina and Mr. Ossory resumed their drive, but for some reason Selina was unable to find the same contentment in Mr. Ossory's presence that she had experienced just moments earlier.

Selina went to her chamber upon her return, thankful to have escaped a meeting with Julia. She wanted to rest before her long evening. Her one experience attending a ball thus far had taught her she should expect to be out until the early hours of the morning.

She pulled back the curtains that surrounded her bed to find Julia lying there, fully clothed and sound asleep.

"Julia," Selina said.

There was no response.

"Julia," Selina said a little louder, reaching out and gently shaking her.

"What?" Julia said, blinking. "Oh," she said, and yawned. "I was waiting for you to return from your drive. Apparently I fell asleep."

"Apparently you did," Selina said.

Julia sat up. "Well, how was it?"

"It was quite pleasant."

"I am sure it was," Julia said. "Mr. Ossory seems like a pleasant young man."

"He is," Selina agreed, crossing her arms over her chest. She wondered what new Machiavellian scheme was circulating under Julia's pretty curls.

"He is not interested in you, is he?"

"Interested in me?" Selina asked.

"Romantically, I mean."

"Of course not."

Julia sighed in relief. "I must say, I am glad to hear that—"

"He is only interested in marrying me because his aunt suggested it," Selina said.

Suzanne Allain

"But he cannot marry you! This will destroy all my plans. How will Mr. Malcolm fall in love with you if you become engaged to someone else?"

"That would make it difficult," Selina agreed.

"You are enjoying this!" Julia said accusingly.

"Oh, Julia, don't worry. I have no intention of becoming engaged to Mr. Ossory." Julia relaxed and began to smile. "Right away," Selina added.

"So you do plan on becoming engaged to him eventually?"

Selina grew serious. "I don't know. I must admit I'd hoped to meet someone in town I might marry, so that I could be in a position to present my younger sisters. It is no secret my parents cannot afford to do so. And I like Mr. Ossory. Don't you?"

Julia became quite interested in examining her nails. "I already said I found him pleasant," she said.

"He is extremely pleasant. And his aunt wanted us to make a match." Selina threw herself on the bed next to Julia. "I already turned down one very advantageous offer, and the gentleman was correct in saying I might not have another opportunity."

"Who was it?"

"A Mr. Woodbury. He's all of sixty-five and quite stout. I felt I could not marry him, even for my family's sake. However, Mr. Ossory is comfortably well off and, as you mentioned, quite presentable. Would it be so wrong of me

50

to marry him, even when I find myself drawn to . . . someone else?"

"I hope you do not mean Mr. Malcolm? It would be folly to allow yourself to have feelings for such a man!" Julia said.

"You are right; he is completely above my touch. He is probably just toying with my affections." Selina looked hopefully at Julia, who just nodded in response. "I suppose, then, I should encourage Mr. Ossory's suit. I like him well enough."

This answer did not appear to please Julia, either. "There is no need to be hasty! Surely you would not want a gentleman to marry you just because his aunt asked him to!"

"I am not sure what I want," Selina said. "Everything is so complicated."

"It *is* complicated," Julia agreed. "And it is all Mr. Malcolm's fault."

Selina rolled her eyes at Julia's propensity for finding fault with Mr. Malcolm, but she could not disagree. Life would not be half so complicated were it not for him.

5

Selina heard a knock at her door just as she was putting the finishing touches on her toilette. Before she had a chance to say anything, the door opened and Julia rushed into the room.

Julia was dressed for the ball in an aquamarine-colored ball gown with a translucent silver overdress. Diamonds glittered around her neck and at her ears. Selina thought she looked like a princess from a fairy tale and told her so.

Julia looked pleased at the compliment. "Thank you. You look very nice as well, but I thought you might want to borrow these for the evening," she said, gesturing to the box in her hand. She opened it, displaying a ruby necklace and earrings.

"They are magnificent," Selina said. "But I could not borrow something so valuable."

"Nonsense," Julia said, removing the necklace from the box and putting it around Selina's neck. "Your neck looks quite bare without it."

Selina had to admit this was true. She had been quite shocked when she first came to town and realized it was the fashion to wear ball gowns with a much lower neckline than she was accustomed to. She loved her bronze ball gown, but there was no denying that the necklace succeeded in covering a great deal of exposed flesh.

"Well, if you are sure," Selina said, looking at her reflection in the mirror with pleasure. She hardly recognized herself. Julia's maid had arranged her hair in a braided coronet at the top of her head with a few tendrils escaping to lie against the nape of her neck. The bronze dress seemed to bring out the fire of her hair and skin, and the ruby necklace added to the richness of her ensemble.

"Thank you, Julia," she said. Every now and again her spoiled school friend surprised her with a sweet gesture.

"'Tis nothing," Julia replied. "We cannot have Mr. Malcolm finding fault with your appearance."

"No, of course not," Selina said, and sighed.

Selina was surprised at how pleased she was to see Cassie that evening. He was escorting them to Lady Hartley's ball, and she had not seen him since he escorted them to her first ball a few evenings previously. She felt like she could relax in his undemanding presence.

Until he stepped on her foot while helping her from the carriage.

Selina cried out in pain while Cassie apologized profusely, Julia castigated him for being a clumsy dolt, and Mrs. Thistlewaite fluttered about helplessly, saying, "Oh, my."

"It is fine," Selina hissed through clenched teeth, realizing their party was attracting attention. "If I could just have your arm, Cassie."

Selina walked as gracefully as she could to the receiving line, trying to put all of her weight on her uninjured foot. As they waited their turn to greet their hostess she was thankful that her long dress hid the fact she was only standing on one foot.

Once they were through the receiving line she sank gratefully into a chair on the edge of the ballroom. She and Julia were immediately surrounded by gentlemen begging them for the first dance, a quadrille. Selina was in a quandary. If she refused any of the gentlemen, she would be unable to dance the rest of the evening, but she felt that she had to rest her foot before the next dance with Mr. Malcolm.

Cassie came to her rescue. "Miss Dalton has promised to sit out this dance with me," he told the other gentlemen.

"Thank you, Cassie," she whispered, gently wiggling her foot back and forth. She had to be able to dance with

Mr. Malcolm; she'd looked forward to it all afternoon. She thought if she just rested her foot through the first set, she would be able to manage the waltz.

Mr. Malcolm approached her as the quadrille was ending and her stomach gave a queer little flip when she saw him. "This is my dance, I believe," he said.

Selina nodded, before rising from her seat and placing her hand on his arm.

"May I say how beautiful you look this evening, Miss Dalton," he said as he led her to the dance floor.

"Yes, you may," Selina said, smiling mischievously at him.

Mr. Malcolm looked surprised at first but then he smiled back. "You are looking extraordinarily beautiful this evening," he said. "There is not a lovelier woman in the room."

"Thank you," Selina said, blushing. "But I was only joking."

"I know you were, but I was not," he said.

The music started and Malcolm swept her into the movements of the dance. For the first few minutes Selina forgot about her injured foot, so caught up was she in the sensation of having Mr. Malcolm's arms around her and his face only inches from her own. But the more they danced the more her foot began to throb until she began to hop lightly whenever the steps of the dance required her to put weight on it.

"Is something the matter?" Malcolm asked her, obviously wondering what had happened to the graceful woman he'd been dancing with only moments before. Selina realized she could not continue bobbing up and down like a bird, and thought perhaps if she allowed Mr. Malcolm to carry more of her weight she would be in less pain. So the hand that had been resting lightly on his shoulder began clutching him tightly, and the few inches between their chests disappeared as Selina began clinging to him like a limpet.

Malcolm felt like someone who had been having a wonderful dream that turned suddenly into a nightmare. One moment he was enjoying a romantic waltz with the most beautiful lady in the room, and the next he found himself intercepting shocked glances from members of the *ton* while whirling the same woman around in a position that would be more acceptable in a boudoir than a ballroom. Something had to be done, and quickly, so he half danced, half dragged Selina through the nearest doorway. They found themselves in a small, dark room, and Malcolm released Selina immediately.

"I don't quite understand. Is something the matter?" he asked her again.

"I'm so sorry," Selina said, taking a step toward him. This proved to be a mistake, as she had stepped forward on her poor, abused foot, which refused to hold her a moment longer. She started to fall, and with a startled cry she reached out and grabbed Mr. Malcolm.

Malcolm once again found himself with Selina thrust

against his chest, but this time he didn't stop to ask why. There was one shaft of light from the partially open door that lit Selina as she stood encircled in his arms. She was looking up at him, her eyes shining, her lips just inches away from his. She was breathing rapidly, her body warm against his, her décolleté evening gown displaying her exquisite charms to his fascinated gaze. He leaned closer, intent on closing the space between their lips, when he heard her say, "My foot."

"What?" he said, drawing back a little.

Selina looked a little dazed. "Cassie stepped on my foot."

"Cassie stepped on your foot," he repeated, and could not believe this was the sort of conversation he was engaged in while holding a beautiful woman in his arms.

"But I was so looking forward to our waltz that I thought if I skipped the quadrille, I would be all right."

"I see," Mr. Malcolm said, and smiled.

They stood there, smiling at each other, Selina still propped against Malcolm's chest. "How does your foot feel now?" he asked her, his head beginning to again lower toward hers.

"I don't feel a thing," she said, before any further speech was made impossible when he covered her mouth with his own.

Malcolm's lips had just brushed Selina's when the door to the room was thrown open. They sprang guiltily apart, although Malcolm remembered to support Selina with his arm. They both stood there, blinking as their eyes tried to adjust to the sudden light, and Malcolm recognized Julia standing there before the door was just as suddenly closed.

"Was that Miss Dalton and Mr. Malcolm?" Malcolm heard a gentleman's voice ask.

"No, of course not. That was Lord and Lady Athingamabotmy," Julia said.

"Pardon?"

"It does not matter who it was. They obviously wished for privacy."

"I thought you said Miss Dalton was in that room," the gentleman said, whose voice Malcolm was beginning to recognize as belonging to Henry Ossory. "She promised me the next dance."

The voices started to fade as the couple walked away and Malcolm attempted to pull Selina back into the circle of his arms. "Sir," she protested, "I think we should return to the ballroom."

"That woman has wretched timing," Malcolm told Selina.

Selina smiled tremulously. "The worst," she agreed.

"Are you sure you want to return to the ballroom?" Malcolm asked, encouraged by that smile. He was acutely aware of his own desires, and they had nothing at all to do with returning to the ballroom.

"It would be the proper thing to do," Selina said.

"That it would, Lady Athingamabotmy," Malcolm said, assisting Selina to the door. He was probably holding her a little closer than was strictly necessary but Selina did not complain. He paused in the doorway and Selina looked up at him. She was leaning against him, her arm under his, and he bent down to say in a lowered voice, "Propriety can be the very devil sometimes."

A very improper tingle formed in Selina's stomach at his intimate tone, and she was forced to concur.

Malcolm led Selina to a chair, then left her to fetch some punch. While he was gone, she was approached by Julia and Mr. Ossory.

"Good evening, Miss Dalton. You are looking quite splendid this evening," Mr. Ossory told Selina.

"Thank you, Mr. Ossory."

"I have come to claim my dance with you."

Before Selina could reply, Julia intervened. "She has hurt her foot and is not dancing this evening."

"But she just danced with Mr. Malcolm," Mr. Ossory protested.

"Exactly. That is how she hurt her foot," Julia lied.

"Then I shall sit this one out with her," Mr. Ossory said to Julia, his pleasant smile beginning to look a little strained.

Julia saw Mr. Malcolm approaching them with a glass of punch in his hand and, turning to Mr. Ossory, said in a loud voice, "Why, thank you, Mr. Ossory, I would love to dance with you."

"What? But I didn't—"

"Sir, there is no need to insist. I already told you I would be pleased to dance with you," Julia said as Mr. Malcolm handed Selina her drink. Julia dragged a bewildered Mr. Ossory, still protesting, onto the dance floor.

Malcolm looked at Selina and smiled. "Perhaps her timing is not so wretched after all," he said.

6

Julia announced over breakfast the next morning her intention to have a dinner party.

"Oh, my dear, I am not sure my poor nerves could stand it. A dinner party, you say?" Mrs. Thistlewaite said.

"It will be fine, Mama. Selina and I will arrange everything."

"Whom do you plan to invite?"

"Oh, I don't know," Julia said with a quick glance at Selina. "Probably just Cassie and his friend Mr. Malcolm, and his friend Mr. Ossory."

"A dinner party only for single gentlemen? Perhaps you should invite some ladies as well."

"But that would make our numbers uneven. What do you think, Selina?" Julia asked her friend, who had been silent during the conversation between Julia and her mother.

She did not immediately respond, so Julia said again, "Selina?"

Selina looked over at Julia. "I beg your pardon, I was not attending. What did you say?"

"I am giving a dinner party and I wondered if you could help with the arrangements," Julia said.

"Of course."

"I must say, it doesn't appear as if your letter contains agreeable news."

"It is from my mother. She has asked me to call on my cousin's widow, Mrs. Covington, while I am in town." Selina wrinkled her nose. "I have only met her once and hoped never to repeat the experience."

"Why? What is wrong with her?"

"Nothing, really, I just find little in common with her. When I met her last I was only fifteen, and she would not accept me at my word that I had no beaux. She quizzed me for twenty minutes on the subject before offering to find me a husband. I hate to think how she'll react if she finds me still unwed at two-and-twenty. She was married, widowed, and married again by that age."

"She sounds dreadfully vulgar. Shall I come with you?" Julia offered.

"If you'd like. She lives in Hans Town."

"What an unfashionable address. I don't think I've ever called on anyone in Hans Town. I wonder what I should wear." Julia looked over to make sure her mother could not hear her, and then whispered to Selina: "Whatever you do, do not mention to Mr. Malcolm that you have such a vulgar cousin. Cassie told me one of his requirements is 'Has genteel relations.'"

"My dear, you must raise your voice. You know my hearing is not what it once was. What are you and Selina whispering about?" Mrs. Thistlewaite asked.

Julia turned to address her mother, raising her voice. "It is nothing, Mama. We are just discussing the arrangements for the dinner party." She turned back to Selina, again lowering her voice. "And as long as we're speaking of it, at the dinner party you will need to sing and play the pianoforte. Musical talent is another item on Mr. Malcolm's list."

"I am surprised Mr. Malcolm desires a wife when he could just as easily hire a performing bear!" Selina replied, her voice rising in anger.

"Oh, no. A performing bear at a dinner party is not at all the thing. Perhaps it would be better if I made the arrangements after all," said Mrs. Thistlewaite.

Selina and Julia were ushered by Mrs. Covington into her small drawing room in her flat in Hans Town. It appeared as if she had taken furnishings from a much larger residence and crammed as many as would fit into her current one. When Selina finally turned her gaze to her cousin, it appeared to Selina as if Mrs. Covington had attempted the same maneuver with her dress. Her massive bosom appeared in grave danger of bursting out of its moorings at any moment.

Mrs. Covington was a widow of eight-and-thirty who wished to appear fifteen years younger and at least two stone lighter. She was dressed in a youthful morning gown of pink and white, with her unnaturally bright hair arranged in ringlets around her face.

"Selina Dalton, as I live and breathe! I have not seen you since my dear Arnie was alive," Mrs. Covington exclaimed.

"How do you do, Mrs. Covington," Selina said.

"Mrs. Covington? Why do you call me Mrs. Covington? You do not have to stand on ceremony with me, young lady. Call me Gertie, as your cousin used to."

"Gertie, please allow me to present to you—"

"Yes, I was just about to ask you who this handsome young lady is. It has taken you long enough to introduce us. Please forgive my cousin, Miss—"

"Thistlewaite," Julia offered.

"Lord, that's a mouthful. Miss Thistlewaite. *Miss Thistlewaite.* Say that one twenty times," Gertie said, laughing loudly.

Julia managed a weak smile in response.

"Where are my manners? Please come, sit down. I was so excited to have callers I practically met you at the door."

Selina and Julia proceeded three feet into the room, Julia stumbling over a small footstool.

"Just kick that out of the way, Miss Thistlewaite. I was forced to economize upon the death of my dear husband three years ago."

"I was so sorry to hear the news of Cousin Arnold's death," Selina said, sitting gingerly on the edge of a small settee, which was backed up against the front of a sofa. Selina wondered what the point was of keeping a sofa that no one was able to sit on.

"Yes, well, it was quite unexpected. He was in the prime of life. The doctor said it was apoplexy. But I say that's what they call everything they can't figure out.

"But enough of such depressing talk. I'm surprised to still be calling you 'miss,' young lady. You must be, what, three-and-twenty?"

"I am twenty-two years old."

"Lord, time flies. I think the last time I saw you you were fifteen. I was sure such a handsome girl would be married by seventeen. Good gracious, by the time I was the age you are now, I'd already buried my first husband. Although, between you and me, it was not such a great loss." Gertie laughed heartily at her own wit, and Selina could have sworn she saw a button pop off the bodice of her cousin's gown.

"Now, Arnie was a different story altogether," Gertie continued. "People told him he'd married below him, but he'd tell them he had me so high on a pedestal that he was leagues below me. That was a very gentlemanly thing to say, and so I always told him. He said it was no more than the truth." Gertie wiped a tear away, and Selina and Julia exchanged an uncomfortable look. Selina tried to repeat her condolences but Gertie went off on another tangent.

Although Selina did very little talking for the next half hour, she did manage to convey her parents' greetings, and then she and Julia prepared to take their leave.

"You cannot mean to leave already?" Gertie asked.

"But, Gertie, we have already stayed long past what is considered polite."

"Oh, you know that I do not care for such things. I haven't even heard about your beaux."

"I am sorry, cousin, I cannot trespass on Miss Thistlewaite's time any longer. But perhaps I can come again another day," Selina was surprised to hear herself say. She had begun to feel sorry for Gertie, who was obviously very lonely and enjoyed having visitors.

"That would be splendid. And I could call on you as well. Where did you say you were staying?"

Selina had purposely avoided saying anything at all about where she was staying, but cornered as she was, she was forced to give the address of the Thistlewaites' town house.

Once they had said their farewells and were safely in the carriage, Julia turned to her friend and said, "You do not actually mean to call upon her again, do you?"

"Yes, I rather think I do. She seemed so very lonely, don't you think?"

"She practically fell upon our necks in joy. She must not get many visitors." Julia and Selina sat a moment in silence. "What she must do is find someone to marry her. She's obviously pining away for another husband."

"What made you think so?" Selina asked, with obvious irony. Gertie had spent almost the entire thirty minutes of their visit discussing men and marriage.

Julia ignored Selina's remark, pursuing her own thoughts. "I am afraid I don't know anyone who would suit her, though. She is so dreadfully vulgar," she finally said.

"But she is pleasant enough," Selina said.

"Yes, I rather liked her. Although I cannot say I am eager to visit her again. I felt in imminent danger of being injured by a precariously placed piece of furniture the entire time."

Selina laughed. "I felt a little as if I were suffocating, myself."

Selina did not feel like laughing when she eventually learned the purpose of Julia's dinner party. It appeared that Cassie had informed Julia that one of the items on Mr. Malcolm's list was "Possesses musical or artistic talent." The dinner party was to be Selina's opportunity to display her talents in that regard.

Selina was sick to death of Malcolm's list. If it hadn't been for that blasted thing, she felt that their mutual attraction would be allowed to take its natural course. With a lady and a gentleman, the natural course was courtship followed by marriage. Without Julia's interference, she would have been able to wholeheartedly enjoy Mr. Malcolm's attentions to her without feeling the whole time that she was participating in some despicable scheme.

Selina hated that feeling. She was by nature very open and honest and she disliked anything that smacked of deception. She particularly disliked the charade Julia had involved her in, and resolved to no longer be a party to it. She wondered what would happen if she failed to meet some requirement on Mr. Malcolm's list. Surely that would bring the foolish game to its end.

Tuesday evening, the date for Julia's dinner party arrived, and Selina was determined to find out.

It was a small party of six: the Thistlewaite ladies, Selina, Lord Cassidy, Mr. Malcolm, and Mr. Ossory. Cassie escorted Mrs. Thistlewaite into dinner, Mr. Malcolm escorted Selina, and Julia followed with Mr. Ossory. Selina was beginning to suspect Julia had a *tendre* for Mr. Ossory. His very appearance on the guest list seemed proof of this, as Julia viewed Mr. Ossory as a threat to her scheme to humiliate Mr. Malcolm, yet she had still invited him. It was unfortunate that Mr. Ossory seemed to consider Julia something of a nuisance and was still intent on courting Selina. However, he did manage to converse politely with

Julia throughout the many courses, only glancing occasionally at Selina, who sat across from him.

Selina was a little shy with Mr. Malcolm, as this was the first time she had encountered him since the evening of that travesty of a waltz and their aborted kiss. She attempted to converse with Cassie, who sat on her right, but he was much too interested in his meal and she was forced to turn back to Malcolm for conversation. Unfortunately, his first question concerned the state of her injured foot.

"It is fine, thank you," she said, blushing furiously.

"That's a pity," Malcolm said, with a wicked smile.

"You found me quite graceful hopping about like a wounded bird, did you?"

"No, not at all. I much preferred it when you ceased the hopping and came home to roost, to continue your bird analogy."

"Perhaps we should not continue this conversation at all," Selina said, giving Mr. Malcolm a warning glance.

"It seems a shame not to when you blush so delightfully, but if you insist, it would be ungentlemanly of me to continue."

"Thank you," Selina said, making a concerted effort not to blush.

There was a slight pause as Malcolm addressed himself to his meal and Selina struggled to regain her composure. Then Malcolm asked: "Since you have ordered me to change the subject, tell me, what is your opinion of the Church Building Act?"

"What a weighty question to ask over soup. I believe it is in bad taste to discuss politics before the entrée is served."

"You are probably correct. However, I would really like to hear your opinion."

Selina looked up at Mr. Malcolm, who was looking very serious all of a sudden. *Why, I do believe he's testing me*, she thought in surprise. She found herself growing a little anxious under his critical gaze and could think of nothing to say. What if she said the wrong thing? What was it he wanted her to say?

Then she felt an energizing spurt of anger followed by a wonderful calm. How dare he sit in judgment of her. She did not care what he thought.

"Well, as the daughter of a clergyman, it is obviously important to me that there are houses of worship available to all. However, I cannot help but feel that the million pounds set aside for this purpose is exorbitant. I believe our government intends by this measure to suppress the radicals and keep anarchy at bay, when they could use some of those funds to better the lot of the poor, thereby accomplishing the same purpose but in a way more truly Christian. I do not suppose that Jesus Christ, who had 'nowhere to lay his head' and who frequently fed the poor, would be pleased with some elaborate structure built in his name while those of its congregation had barely enough to eat."

Selina had grown impassioned during her speech and,

realizing that her voice had begun to rise, broke off in some embarrassment and looked over at Malcolm. "I apologize for the lecture, but you did ask my opinion."

"And I should have known better than to ask the daughter of a clergyman. I am sure your father himself could not preach a more eloquent sermon," he told her, smiling.

"What is your opinion?"

"Very much the same, actually," Malcolm said. "Although I do not think I could have begun to express it as well as you did."

Selina, sensing the approval in his gaze, realized she'd passed his test. She was pleased for a moment, until she remembered that she had begun the evening with the resolve to *fail* to meet his requirements.

She reminded herself of this once again when the gentlemen rejoined the ladies after dinner and Julia announced that there should be music.

"Selina, would you honor us with a song?" Julia asked.

"I am sorry, Julia, but I have no musical ability whatsoever. It would be a punishment to force you all to listen to me."

There were quite varying reactions to Selina's calm pronouncement. Cassie looked pleased, as he felt it a punishment to have to listen to any lady perform on the pianoforte, skilled or not. Mr. Ossory looked his same agreeable self; he actually smiled at Selina's admission. Mr. Malcolm looked a little displeased, Selina thought, perhaps even surprised. Julia, of course, looked cross, but managed a little chuckle.

"Oh, Selina, you are quite the joker. Of course you have musical ability. I heard you play myself just yesterday. She is quite talented," she assured Mr. Malcolm.

Selina thought about arguing further, but Julia appeared implacable in her determination to have Selina perform and Selina did not feel she should cause a scene. There was no other option than for her to play for the company. *But*, she told herself as she took her seat at the pianoforte, *that does not mean I have to play well*.

She launched into a Beethoven sonata, determined to miss most of her notes, but she found that such a thing was easier said than done. Her fingers automatically flew over the keys, playing the notes that she'd memorized and were second nature to her, and she was halfway through before realizing it was too late to succeed in convincing people she did not know how to play.

When she finished, she looked sheepishly at her audience. Cassie, who had taken her at her word when she said that she had no musical ability, tried to console her. "That was not so bad," he said, smiling encouragingly at her.

"My dear fellow, it was not bad at all. It was superb," Malcolm said. "But, Miss Dalton, I do not understand. Why did you try to convince us you have no talent? Do you have such an aversion to performing before others?"

"No, it is not that," Selina said, wondering how to explain her bizarre behavior. "I just thought that if I claimed to have talent, I was sure to disappoint, but if I claimed no talent, any performance I gave was bound to be acceptable."

"It was quite acceptable," Mr. Ossory told her. "Let us have another."

"No, no. It is Julia's turn to perform," Selina said, turning to her friend. "Perhaps you would like to sing for us? Julia has a beautiful singing voice," Selina told the others.

Julia modestly demurred, but it was obvious she was not truly averse to the idea. This was her opportunity to shine before Mr. Ossory. She was a talented singer, and Selina thought she made a pretty picture as she sang before them, accompanying herself on the pianoforte.

Selina's thoughts had been so full of Mr. Malcolm she had given scant consideration to her conversation with Mr. Ossory. She wondered if she was making a mistake in not encouraging him. He was obviously an estimable young gentleman, and Selina thought she would have a very comfortable life with him. She turned from her contemplation of him to look at Mr. Malcolm, who was staring at her, and her heart began an accelerated rhythm that had been noticeably absent when she had been observing Mr. Ossory. And all of a sudden the thought of having a "comfortable life" was very unsatisfying.

7

The day following the dinner party, Julia, Selina, and Cassie sat in the Thistlewaites' drawing room, discussing their successful entertainment of the previous evening. Selina felt a strange sense of having lived through this moment before, and was reminded of their first meeting three weeks earlier upon her arrival in town. It seemed a long time ago that they sat in this very room and talked about their plan of captivating Mr. Malcolm.

And now Selina felt *she* was the one whose heart was in danger.

However, Julia was extremely optimistic about their progress thus far, and even Cassie, who would have loved to contradict his cousin, believed his friend was smitten with Selina. Cassie told the ladies that Malcolm had spoken very highly of Selina following the dinner party.

"He said that he admired her prodigiously. He had first been impressed by her wit and humor, but was concerned that she was not serious enough, which augured an unsteady character. But he said after last night that fear had been laid to rest."

" 'Not serious enough. An unsteady character.' He certainly makes rash judgments," Selina said, annoyed. "What, was I to launch into a political debate in the middle of a ball?"

"You see, Selina, it is just as I told you. There is no pleasing the man. If you had not joked with him, he would have been sure to castigate you as lacking in humor," Julia said.

Cassie realized that once again he'd managed to put his foot in it. "I have probably quoted him incorrectly. Sometimes he uses such long words . . . He was very complimentary. He said that Selina had met nearly all of the qualifications on his list, but there were a few others that he needed to test her on."

"So this is what I have to look forward to, is it? To be tested by Mr. Malcolm?" Selina asked.

Before Cassie could reply, they were interrupted by Reeves's announcement of a caller.

"Mrs. Covington," Reeves intoned.

"Good morning, good morning," Gertie said as she bustled into the room. She was resplendent in a peach frock cut indecently low for afternoon wear, her blond hair covered with a huge bonnet bedecked with flowers.

"Cousin Gertie. How nice to see you again," Selina said, looking at Julia for direction.

"Please sit down, Mrs. Covington," Julia said.

"I thought we agreed it was to be Gertie, and you're to be Julia. Heaven knows I can hardly say your last name without spitting, although I suppose I shouldn't admit to it."

Selina rather thought it would have been better had she not, but before she had a chance to offer any opinion at all, Cassie drew attention to himself with a little cough, and Julia introduced him to Gertie.

Gertie was struck dumb for a full thirty seconds when she discovered she was in the presence of a lord, and into the unusual silence Reeves announced another caller.

"The Honorable Mr. Malcolm," he said.

"Good heavens! An honorable *and* a lord," Gertie exclaimed loudly, and Selina felt a twinge of embarrassment on her behalf.

Julia once again performed the introductions, and Mr. Malcolm proclaimed himself honored to make Mrs. Covington's acquaintance.

"Oh, no, sir, it is I who is honored. I have never been in the same room with a lord and an honorable. Though I'm not exactly sure what it means to be an honorable. It's the next best thing to being a lord, right?"

"I am the younger son of an earl," Malcolm said, looking a little taken aback.

"Now, that's a real pity. Because you've got the look of a lord, much more so than this young gentleman here," Gertie said, gesturing toward Cassie. "No offense, my lord. You seem a good sort, but Mr. Malcolm has a more dignified look about him."

"It's all right. I know I'm not the dignified type," Cassie said.

Julia decided it was time someone took control of the situation. "Cassie, Mrs. Covington would probably enjoy going for a drive. I do not believe she gets out very much and she would enjoy such an excursion, would you not, Mrs. Covington?"

"That would be a fair treat, but his lordship may have other plans for the afternoon."

Cassie started to nod, but encountered a commanding look from Julia. "Not—not at all. I would be pleased to take you for a spin."

"Well, thank you kindly. I am glad I dressed so sensibly today. I was going to wear a different gown, but I decided it looked a little too immature. There is nothing worse than a woman in her midtwenties dressing like a debutante."

No one knew what to say to such an obvious falsehood, so Cassie finally broke the silence by suggesting they take their leave.

"Of course, of course. One thing I learned after two trips to the altar is that the gentlemen don't like to be kept waiting. Julia, Selina, I'll call again sometime soon."

"We look forward to it," Selina said, and Cassie and Gertie left the room.

"How are you acquainted with Mrs. Covington?" Malcolm asked the ladies once Gertie was gone.

"She is—" Selina started to say.

"My cousin," Julia interrupted.

Selina looked at Julia in confusion, wondering why she would claim Gertie as a relative when Selina was hesitant to do so herself.

"Cousin by marriage, that is," Julia clarified.

"I see. Does her presence here indicate you have decided to introduce her into society?" Mr. Malcolm asked.

"Oh, no. No, of course not. I just realized that she was lonely since the death of Cousin—"

"Arnold," Selina whispered.

"Arnold," Julia continued. "So I paid her a call and invited her to do the same. I did not want her sitting at home alone."

A strained silence descended upon the inhabitants of the drawing room. Malcolm had come to invite Selina to go driving with him, but felt uncomfortable doing so in the face of Julia's remark that she did not want Mrs. Covington sitting at home alone. Selina was still annoyed with Malcolm because of the remarks he'd made to Cassie, and Julia was wondering how she could maneuver Malcolm and Selina into a position where they could be alone together.

Mrs. Thistlewaite came into the drawing room at that

moment, a little surprised to find herself the focus of all attention.

"Oh, excuse me," she said, as if she'd stumbled into someone else's drawing room and not her own. "I did not mean to intrude."

"It is perfectly all right, Mrs. Thistlewaite. I am about to take my leave," Malcolm said, before turning to Selina. "I wonder, Miss Dalton, if you would like to go driving with me?"

"Oh. That would be lovely," Selina said, a little less than enthusiastically.

Mr. Malcolm looked at Selina searchingly before saying, "You do not have to go if you do not want to."

"Of course I want to. Let me just get my hat," she said, rising and leaving the room. Julia excused herself as well to follow Selina to her chamber.

"Selina," Julia said once they were in Selina's chamber. "Do not tell Malcolm that Gertie is your cousin. One of the items on his list is 'Has genteel relations.'"

"So that is why you claimed her as your cousin. I must admit I found that a little strange."

"Yes, well, I thought it was the wisest thing to do. So do not mention anything to the contrary to Mr. Malcolm."

"I will not, Julia," Selina said, putting on her bonnet. "I promise to be everything he desires in a woman: witty, humorous, serious, sober, genteel, musical . . . all at the same time."

"Excellent," Julia said.

Selina let out an exasperated moan and Julia looked at her in surprise. "Selina, is something the matter?"

"No, of course not, what could be the matter? I am merely preparing for my role."

Julia finally realized that Selina was being less than sincere. "I know this is not pleasant for you, Selina, but I think it should be over soon."

"Yes, I know. I am not sure if that is my greatest hope or my worst fear," Selina said with a sigh and, checking her appearance one last time in the mirror, left the room.

She and Mr. Malcolm passed the first few minutes of the drive in silence, Mr. Malcolm finally saying, "You are very quiet this afternoon."

"I beg your pardon," Selina said. "The weather this afternoon is quite lovely, is it not?" she said, making an attempt to appear in better spirits.

Malcolm looked up at the sky, which was filled with ominous-looking dark clouds. "Please do not feel that you have to make conversation. I much prefer silence to those that ramble on with nothing to say, like that Mrs. Covington. She was quite a character, was she not? I am glad I am not courting Miss Thistlewaite."

"I beg your pardon? What do you mean by that?"

Malcolm looked a little surprised at the vehemence of

Selina's tone. "Nothing, really. I mean it's rather obvious, isn't it, that I would want my future wife's relations to possess a modicum of gentility."

"And if they did not?" Selina asked.

"Why, you look quite fierce. I do not understand why you are so upset; it is a moot point, after all. I am not courting Julia Thistlewaite, I am courting—" He paused, looking a little self-conscious. "Well, I think it's fairly obvious who it is I am courting, isn't it?"

"But if you were courting Julia and you had met Mrs. Covington, would it affect your opinion of Julia?"

"Well, it would have to, would it not? I mean, that *is* something you have to consider when contemplating marriage with someone." Malcolm looked over at Selina, who was frowning. "Why do you look so grim? Do not tell me you have a relation as vulgar as Mrs. Covington?"

Selina forced a smile. "No, I would not tell you that." *Not after Julia forbade me to,* Selina thought.

"I am pleased to hear it."

They had reached the park, and Mr. Malcolm nodded at someone in a passing carriage but did not stop. He looked over at Selina, wondering if he should take her home. It was obvious she was displeased with him. Perhaps she thought his attitude toward Mrs. Covington arrogant. But she had seemed out of sorts even before that. He was struck suddenly with the thought that she might not like him. It was a novel idea, so accustomed was he to females of all kinds fawning over him. For the first time it occurred to him that even if she passed all the items on his list, she may not accept his suit.

She was looking exceptionally beautiful that afternoon in her russet-colored carriage dress, which just matched her hair. Her beauty shocked him each time he saw her, although she was not the most beautiful woman he'd ever known. It was more than just her outward appearance he found so appealing, although he had to admit he found it very appealing indeed. But he was attracted also by her traits of character: her vitality, her humor, her intelligence, her kindness. She was everything he desired in a woman. He wondered suddenly what it was that she desired in a man.

"Why did you come to London, Miss Dalton?" he asked her.

She looked a little startled at the sudden question, and there was a slight pause as she thought it over. "Because I was lonely," she finally said.

"That's interesting," Mr. Malcolm said, and Selina looked over at him. "I was lonely before you came to London, too."

Selina smiled in response and Malcolm felt as if the sun had finally come out, although it was still as cloudy as ever.

"I am having a house party at my estate in Kent, and I would be pleased if you would come," he said.

"I am honored by the invitation, but I am a guest of the Thistlewaites—"

"Oh, I will invite them as well. And Cassie, of course."

"And Mr. Ossory?"

"If you would like," Malcolm said, a little displeased that she thought of him so quickly. "My mother is coming to act as hostess. I thought perhaps your parents might like to come as well."

"Thank you. I shall write and ask them," Selina said.

"If you give me their direction, I would be pleased to send an invitation."

Selina supplied the information, although she was a little ambivalent about the house party. Her parents would be sure to think she was on the verge of matrimony were they to receive an invitation to the house party of a man they had never met. Things were moving very fast, and Selina was afraid the climax was going to come just as swiftly. And while she was involved in this stupid scheme of Julia's, she was sure that the ending would not be a happy one.

The rest of the drive passed more amicably than it had at the beginning, and Selina began to forget her former annoyance with Mr. Malcolm and feel a return of her previous feelings for him. She sincerely enjoyed his company. And when he grasped her by the waist to help her down from the curricle, she realized again the force of her physical attraction to him. She felt a nervous excitement around him that she had never before felt in her twenty-two years.

But then something occurred that brought a return of Selina's previous ambivalence. When Malcolm finally released her and she turned to walk toward the house, she discovered that her dress had somehow found its way under his foot. There was a loud ripping sound and Selina looked in dismay at the torn ruffle at the bottom of her dress.

Malcolm immediately apologized, and when Selina looked up at him to assure him it was all right, she began to wonder if he had planned the entire incident. He did not look surprised or sorry, but rather was looking at her in a quizzical manner, as if judging her reaction.

Is this another of his stupid tests? Selina thought to herself as she continued on to the house while assuring him once again that it was nothing.

"I am sorry to be so clumsy, but I am relieved to see you have forgiven me so readily," Mr. Malcolm told her.

"Oh, I am not one to hold a grudge, particularly over such a small matter as a torn ruffle," Selina said, and when Malcolm broke into a huge smile, she realized that once again she had passed one of the criteria on that blasted list.

8

Mr. Malcolm accompanied Selina into the drawing room and extended an invitation to his house party to Julia and Mrs. Thistlewaite before taking his leave. Julia was pleased to hear about the house party, particularly when she found out Mr. Ossory was going to be invited as well.

"You will be quite impressed with Hadley Hall, Selina," Julia said. "It was built a hundred years ago in the Palladian style and has an immense entrance hall that is considered one of the finest classical rooms in all of England."

"It sounds quite impressive. Have you been there?"

"No, I have not; I have only read about it. However, I have always longed to see it. Now I shall have the opportunity."

Julia did not seem to feel any twinges of guilt about accepting hospitality from a man upon whom she was scheming to avenge herself. Selina could only reflect that it must be convenient to have such an easy conscience. She herself viewed the visit with a good deal of apprehension.

But she could not deny she felt a certain curiosity as well. She would meet Mr. Malcolm's mother and see his estate. In such a setting they were bound to spend more time together than they had enjoyed in London. She would finally be able to discover if Malcolm was the arrogant scoundrel Julia insisted he was, and which he sometimes gave evidence of being, or if he was the man of her dreams, which she often thought he was as well.

Selina wondered if she would have felt differently about Mr. Malcolm if she had not known about the list. She had to admit to herself that she would. If one was unaware one was being measured like a pair of shoes, it would not have been so disconcerting. After all, Selina was matching him to a set of criteria, although not as overtly. She, too, had qualifications she desired her future husband to meet. That was not arrogant; it was practical.

And so far Mr. Malcolm had exceeded all of Selina's requirements but one: she required humility in a husband.

Julia told Selina there was one last ball she wanted them to attend before leaving town. "Normally I would not care to go, as it is given by Lady Cynthia Sommers, who everyone knows is becoming desperate in her efforts to find a husband, but I asked Mr. Malcolm if he would be there and he said he would, and so we should go as well."

"And will Mr. Ossory be there?" Selina asked.

"I believe he mentioned he would be. What a bother that man has become. I will have to distract him once again or he'll be sure to monopolize you completely."

"I appreciate your efforts on my behalf," Selina said. Julia, who either did not recognize the sarcasm in Selina's tone or refused to acknowledge it, just replied that it was nothing.

Selina was not disappointed to have to attend one last ball. She enjoyed dancing very much, and the balls she had attended upon her arrival in town put the small assemblies in her home village to shame. The assembly rooms in Bath were very beautiful, but it was not Mrs. Ossory's habit to attend, so Selina had only been once. Julia told Selina that there was a ball every night in London during the season, and it was the custom to take in two or three entertainments in one evening, so Julia found the current entertainments paltry in comparison. But Selina was unused to such a pleasure-seeking lifestyle and was glad she hadn't arrived at the height of the season. She could look forward to each ball with excitement, rather than ennui.

She was definitely looking forward to tonight's ball. But she had to admit that if Mr. Malcolm were not attending, she would not be feeling such anticipation.

Their party was greeted by Lady Cynthia and her parents, and Selina wondered why the lady was so desperate to make a match when she was so very beautiful. But the lady's beauty was marred to some extent by her haughty expression, and Selina thought it was perhaps her character that ruined her chances. The only person in the group Lady Cynthia smiled at was Cassie, who blushed and ducked his head. Selina realized Julia had spoken no more than the truth: none but the most desperate of women would smile at Cassie so seductively.

Selina had just entered the ballroom when she was approached by Mr. Malcolm. She realized he had been waiting for her to arrive, and she was thrilled by this evidence of his regard. She felt more and more like she could let down the careful guard over her heart and give it into his keeping. It certainly appeared as if he genuinely liked her. Particularly when he looked at her as he did now.

"Good evening, Miss Dalton," he said, bowing low over her hand.

"Mr. Malcolm," she replied, dropping a curtsy.

"May I have this dance?"

"I would be delighted."

Selina was not as delighted when she realized it was a quadrille that was being formed; she had been hoping for a waltz. Still, she enjoyed dancing, particularly with Mr. Malcolm, and greeted Julia and Cassie with a smile when they joined their set. Another couple joined whom Selina was not familiar with, and then Lady Cynthia arrived with a rather unkempt middle-aged gentleman. Selina was a little dismayed that she would be forced to clasp hands with him.

But when the music started, she forgot all about Lady Cynthia and her partner. She found this quadrille different from any she'd ever danced. Malcolm followed the steps of the dance perfectly, but it was clear that his attention was primarily for Selina. It suddenly seemed an elaborate game of cat and mouse, being whisked away from Mr. Malcolm only to be returned to him again, the grip of his hand warm and steady, his gaze only leaving hers when the steps of the dance separated them. Selina found herself smiling with pure joy. She failed to notice Lady Cynthia's darkening countenance.

When the dance ended, Mr. Malcolm led her from the floor. He said very little, merely promenading with her around the perimeter of the ballroom. He finally led her to a chair that was half hidden by a pillar. "Please wait here," he said. "I am going to get you something to drink. I should probably return you to Mrs. Thistlewaite, but I think I am going to act selfishly and keep you all to myself for a little while."

"I must be selfish as well, because I can find no fault with your plan," Selina said. Mr. Malcolm smiled, raised her hand to his lips, and left.

Selina stared dreamily into space, letting the sounds of

music and conversation waft over her, until the mention of Malcolm's name and then her own made her sit up in startled attention.

"What think you of Mr. Malcolm's attentions to Miss Dalton?" a man asked, though Selina missed the first part of his question. She did not miss the very haughty "Harrumph" from the person so addressed.

"You must be joking. Mr. Malcolm and Miss Dalton?" There was a delighted trill of laughter. Selina leaned forward to look around the pillar and noticed with some surprise that the speakers were barely ten feet in front of her. They were Lord Sylvester Mountjoy and Lady Cynthia Sommers. "She's a complete nonentity," Lady Cynthia continued. "Her father is a country vicar. Everyone knows how fastidious Mr. Malcolm is. He is obviously trifling with her for his own amusement."

"Methinks the lady doth protest too much," Lord Sylvester said, but Selina could no longer see him. She had leaned back behind the pillar, all of a sudden overcome with embarrassment at the thought they might see her.

She did not know why she should be embarrassed for them to know she'd overheard their comments; if she had any spirit at all, she would stand up and confront them, but she worried that what Lady Cynthia said was all too true. And though she might wish to believe Malcolm was enamored of her, how could she know the true state of his affections?

"Miss Dalton."

Selina looked up, startled, to see Mr. Malcolm standing before her, a glass of punch in his hand. She wondered how much, if anything, he'd overheard. Surely he'd just arrived? Perhaps he'd heard nothing.

"Mr. Malcolm. Thank you for fetching the punch. I find myself quite thirsty after that lively dance," Selina said, reaching for the drink. She was shocked when Mr. Malcolm set it on the floor and grabbed her hands, kneeling before her.

"Miss Dalton, please do not be dismayed by what you just heard."

"I'm sure I don't know what you mean," Selina said, unable to meet Malcolm's eyes and attempting to withdraw her hands from his grasp.

"Do not bother to pretend. I heard Lady Cynthia saying that I was merely trifling with you, and if I heard it, you must have heard it as well. It is not true."

"Isn't it?" Selina asked, giving up on her attempts to free her hands and meeting Mr. Malcolm's gaze. He did not look away.

"No, it is not. I know that I have such a reputation—we have even discussed it before—but you have nothing to fear from me. I value your esteem too much to risk losing it. In fact, I wonder if it is not I who should be afraid."

"Nonsense. What do you have to fear?" Selina whispered.

"It scares me that with the mere touch of your pretty hand"—he stopped and raised said hand to his lips—"my heart goes into strong convulsions." He pressed her hand against his chest, but Selina's own heart was beating so rapidly she could not tell if the staccato thumping she felt was his or her own. "Such a thing cannot be healthy, do you think?" Mr. Malcolm asked her. Selina could only shake her head. "But even more terrifying is the thought that as suddenly as you appeared in the library that night, you could disappear. That I could wake up one morning to find that you were 'a lovely apparition sent to be a moment's ornament.' For you seem too perfect to be real."

"You worry needlessly, sir. I am far from perfect, and only too real."

"Perhaps I should feel the beat of your heart, so I can confirm that," Mr. Malcolm said, reaching out a hand toward her chest.

"Mr. Malcolm!" Selina exclaimed, drawing back from his hand. Then she saw the laughter in his eyes.

"It seemed a fair exchange," he said.

"You will just have to take my word for it," Selina said, trying to refrain from smiling.

"Hmmm. I suppose I will. For now, anyway," Malcolm said, rising from his kneeling position and holding out his arm to her. Selina rose from her seat, too flustered to think of a response.

Hadley Hall was less than a day's drive from London, in the Kentish Weald. It was not far from the Sussex border, so it would also be a convenient drive for Selina's parents. Selina could feel her stomach knotting in anticipation as the carriage turned into the long drive that led to Hadley Hall.

Mrs. Thistlewaite had fallen asleep, which in Selina's opinion was a very good thing. She had fretted for the first few hours of the trip, convinced that she had left something behind but unsure exactly what. Julia and Selina had formed a tacit agreement not to wake her, and so the last portion of the trip was spent in silence. Selina herself was too nervous to fall asleep, and as the carriage approached the hall, she stared out the window in fascination.

She saw a beautifully landscaped park and man-made lake, flanked by a Palladian-style mansion in yellow brick. The enormity of the place astounded her, and when she was let down from the carriage, she could only look around in awe. Mrs. Thistlewaite had finally woken up, and she stumbled out of the carriage, followed by Julia.

"Is it not impressive?" Julia asked Selina.

"Indeed it is," Selina said. "I feel like I've been transported to Rome."

It was an unusually hot day, even for July, and the weather contributed further to Selina's impression of having been magically conveyed to another time and place. Before anything more could be said, Mr. Malcolm came out of the hall and met them at the bottom of the steps.

"I am pleased to welcome you to my home," he told the three ladies, but it was obvious it was Selina he was delighted to see.

"It is very beautiful," Selina told him.

"Thank you. I hope you will find the interior just as beautiful. May I escort you inside?" he asked, offering his arm to Selina, with Julia and Mrs. Thistlewaite following.

He escorted them into the entrance hall, a fifty-foot-high room with a coved and coffered ceiling supported by alabaster columns. There were busts of Greek and Roman gods in niches around the room.

"The ceiling is from a design by Inigo Jones," Mr. Malcolm told them, and Selina managed a nod in response.

The housekeeper had met them at the door, and Mr. Malcolm asked her to show the ladies to their rooms. "My mother is awaiting you in the Grand Salon, but I thought you might like to refresh yourselves before joining her."

"That would be lovely," Selina said, and Julia and Mrs. Thistlewaite agreed.

The ladies had just started to walk away when Mr. Malcolm called, "Miss Dalton."

Selina turned back to speak to Mr. Malcolm. "Yes?"

"Your parents will be arriving tomorrow," he told her. He smiled tenderly at her, lowered his voice a little, and said, "I am very happy that you are here." His smile was not in the least bit arrogant. In fact, he looked quite a bit more relaxed and contented than he'd ever appeared in town.

"I am very happy to be here as well," Selina told him before rejoining the other ladies.

Selina found herself in a very pretty room with a view of the lake. It was called the Blue Room, and was papered in a blue-and-white toile with matching bed linens. There was a little window seat that Selina sank into once she had supervised the unpacking of her things and was alone.

Never in her wildest imaginings could she have invented such a place. She had known Mr. Malcolm was wealthy, and even that he was the possessor of a fine estate, but the reality of those words had not made an impression on her until today. She suddenly realized what it meant to be the recipient of attentions from such a man.

Selina had had a modest upbringing, but it was not a sheltered one. Her family was not wealthy, but neither had they lacked for anything, and they had enjoyed the patronage of Lord Musgrove, a distant relation and the granter of the parish post where her father served. She had felt as at home in his manor house as she had at the vicarage. Then, when she left the small village to serve as Mrs. Ossory's companion, she had lived in an elegant town house, and was acquainted through Mrs. Ossory with gentlemen and ladies of wealth and prestige.

But Hadley Hall was more luxurious than anything she had ever seen. So much wealth was intimidating to Selina. And the thought that Mr. Malcolm believed her to be a fit mistress for such a place was a humbling one.

She heard a knock at the door. "Come in," she said.

The door opened. "Selina, it is time to go down for tea," Julia told her.

"Already?" Selina protested, but rose from her seat. "I was hoping I could stay in that window seat forever."

Julia did not reply for a moment, as she was busy looking around her. "I do believe your room is larger than mine," she finally said.

"Perhaps he wanted to put you next to your mother," Selina suggested.

"Perhaps," Julia replied, but Selina knew that Julia counted it as another mark against Mr. Malcolm.

Selina wished once again that her friend had not taken such a dislike to Malcolm, but realized it was useless to argue with her on the subject. Mrs. Thistlewaite was waiting for them outside the door, and the three ladies were met by a footman at the base of the stairs who directed them to the salon.

The walls of the salon were covered in a rich crimson velvet, on which numerous paintings were hung. The effect was quite opulent, but Selina did not find it to her taste. She preferred the classicism of the entrance hall and the elegant rusticity of her bedchamber. Before she could make any further impressions, she was distracted from her perusal of the room by Mr. Malcolm rising to meet them.

Selina found her heart was beating uncomfortably fast as Mr. Malcolm introduced her and the Thistlewaites to his mother, Lady Kilbourne.

Lady Kilbourne was a handsome, elegant woman of middle years. Her hair was now gray, but Selina thought at one time it had probably been as dark as her son's. She had the same coloring as him, including his brown eyes. Lady Kilbourne smiled kindly at Selina, but Selina felt irrationally intimidated by her. She was *too* elegant, making Selina instantly aware of all the defects of her toilette. Mr. Malcolm's mother sat straight-backed on the sofa, her expression hidden by half-closed eyelids. The ladies were invited to sit, and were offered some tea. All of this was done in a languid manner, as if the whole process fatigued Lady Kilbourne greatly. Selina took some bread and butter, and then wished she had not, as she was too nervous to eat anything.

"Miss Dalton, my son tells me you were raised in Sussex," Lady Kilbourne said.

"Yes, my lady."

"What part of Sussex?"

"A small village near Chailey," Selina said. She wished Julia or Mrs. Thistlewaite would contribute something to the conversation.

"And your father is still serving as vicar there, I believe."

"Yes, my lady."

"And your mother? Are her people from Sussex as well?"

"Yes, my lady," Selina said a third time, feeling like a complete fool. "Her family's name is Kingswater," she offered, glad she was finally able to make a comment that was not in direct response to a question.

"Kingswater," Lady Kilbourne repeated, looking thoughtful. "I am afraid I do not know any Kingswaters," she finally said, and took a sip of tea.

Selina did not know how to respond. She felt somehow to blame for Lady Kilbourne's lack of knowledge of her mother's family. Thankfully, Lady Kilbourne turned to the Thistlewaites and began speaking to them. Selina was grateful for the reprieve and made an effort to eat some bread and butter.

She made little contribution to the rest of the teatime conversation, which she thought was probably fortunate considering her poor demonstration of wit so far. After tea, Mr. Malcolm asked if any of the ladies would like a tour of the house.

Mrs. Thistlewaite and Julia declined, mentioning they would like to rest before dinner.

"And you, Miss Dalton?" Mr. Malcolm asked, looking at Selina.

Selina looked over at Lady Kilbourne, who was smiling pleasantly at her, but still with her eyes half-closed. "Yes, I would enjoy a tour of the house," Selina said rather hesitantly. She did not want to appear forward. "I have never seen a house like Hadley Hall," she explained to Lady Kilbourne.

"There is not another house like it," Lady Kilbourne said.

"Well, then," Mr. Malcolm said, rising. "Shall we begin the tour?"

Selina rose and excused herself to the others. Lady Kilbourne reminded them not to take too long, as dinner would be served promptly at seven.

They began their tour in the Statue Gallery, a long, narrow room lined with windows that were filled with marble statues.

"This is my favorite room in the house," Mr. Malcolm told her. "When we have a large entertainment, such as a ball, we serve supper here."

"It is quite beautiful," Selina said, admiring the bright room, which was lit by the afternoon sun. It was a good deal less fussy than the salon, and Selina felt herself relaxing a little.

They walked slowly the length of the room, pausing to examine a statue every so often. They stopped before one objet d'art for a few minutes, and Selina eventually realized Mr. Malcolm was observing her rather than it.

"Are you sure you're quite comfortable?" Mr. Malcolm asked Selina when she turned to meet his stare. "You have not reinjured your foot, I hope?"

"No, not at all, I am fine. Why do you ask?"

"You did not seem yourself at tea. The only other time I have known you to act so curiously you were suffering from an injury."

Selina smiled. "I wish I could complain of an injury to my tongue, which might explain why I was unable to speak in anything other than monosyllables, but I do not have such an excuse, I am afraid. I was suffering from nothing more than a fit of shyness."

"That is odd. You have never struck me as the shy sort before."

"Well, you must admit all of this magnificence is rather intimidating," Selina said, with a wide gesture that took in the room.

"I can see how it might be," Mr. Malcolm said, but when Selina looked up at him, she found he was staring at her.

"I do not believe that anything intimidates you," Selina said.

"Do I seem so fearsome a presence, then?"

"Yes."

Malcolm laughed. "Oh, come now, surely you exaggerate. I cannot be that intimidating. My niece and nephew adore me, and they are only five and six. If I do not scare little children, there can be nothing in my appearance to frighten a young lady of—what, twenty-five?"

"Twenty-two!" Selina said, a little upset that he thought her older than she was.

"Have I offended you with my guess?" Malcolm asked. "It is a little stratagem I've developed to discover a lady's true age. If you guess too high, they will always blurt out the truth, whereas if you ask them directly, they are usually reluctant to tell you."

"You are very crafty. I can see I will have to be on my guard with you at all times."

"Not at all. I am unwise enough to give away my little secrets. You have nothing to fear from me. A true manipulator would not have told you that you had been manipulated," Mr. Malcolm said, smiling in a manner that Selina felt was very manipulative indeed. She was certain he could get nearly anything he wanted with a flash of that smile.

"I see you have worked this all out in your mind so that you have an excuse for any behavior," Selina said.

"Precisely. For example, if I tell you that I manipulated you into taking this tour so that I might steal a kiss, then I have not been truly devious, for I have admitted my design to you."

Selina felt her heart beating a little quicker, even though Mr. Malcolm had made no effort to touch her. Still, she managed a light response. "But then your plan is doomed to failure, because now I have been forewarned and I can protect myself from your advances."

"*Is* my plan doomed to failure?" Mr. Malcolm said, putting his arm around Selina's waist.

"Yes, of course," Selina said, before melting into Mr. Malcolm's arms.

This kiss was altogether more satisfying than their first one at Lady Hartley's ball. That night, Malcolm's lips had barely touched hers, and his arms had been around her much too briefly. Now she was ensconced in such a firm embrace she could feel the solid bulk of his chest pressed against hers. This time his lips touched hers firmly and remained there until she felt in danger of collapsing from either lack of air or because of the sudden weakness she felt in her lower extremities, she was not sure which.

Before she fell victim to either, Malcolm raised his head. "You forgot to protect yourself," he told Selina.

"What?" she asked.

"I gave you fair warning I meant to steal a kiss, so I cannot be held accountable for my actions."

"So you did," Selina said, rallying a little. "I suppose, then, that I am forced to forgive you."

"Good. Because that is the last time I intend to warn you," he said, and kissed her again.

Selina was hard put to answer that evening at dinner when Lady Kilbourne asked her what part of the tour she'd enjoyed most. She intercepted a wicked glance from Mr. Malcolm, and could feel herself turning red.

"I believe it was the Statue Gallery that you found most delightful, was it not?" Mr. Malcolm said.

"I did enjoy the Statue Gallery," Selina said, before realizing how Mr. Malcolm would interpret her words. "That is, I found the Statue Gallery most pleasing." Malcolm's grin widened. "The marbles were exquisite," Selina said, thankful she had finally said something that could not be misinterpreted by Mr. Malcolm.

"And which figure did you most admire?" Malcolm asked her.

"Jeremy!" his mother chided him. "Can't you see you are embarrassing Miss Dalton?" Lady Kilbourne turned to Selina. "Do not worry, Miss Dalton. You are not the first to find the statues somewhat shocking. While my sister was alive, she gave a tour of the house and one of the ladies later said that it was a pity that there was not some contrivance that could be hit upon to conceal the nudity of the males, for lady spectators were rather nonplussed when viewing them."

Selina smiled at Lady Kilbourne, thankful that she had come to her defense, even though it was not the statues she found embarrassing, but rather Mr. Malcolm's veiled references to the kisses he'd stolen.

However, Selina's modesty seemed to impress Lady Kilbourne (or perhaps it was her ability to converse in full sentences that did the trick), because Lady Kilbourne's chill seemed to thaw by the time dinner was over. When everyone retired to the drawing room after dinner, Lady Kilbourne requested that Selina play for them.

"My son tells me you're quite an accomplished young lady," Lady Kilbourne said, smiling at Selina.

Selina acquiesced with good grace, although she hurried to suggest Julia as the next performer once she'd finished her piece. It was obvious to Selina that Julia was becoming irritated with all the special attention that Selina was receiving.

9

The following afternoon the rest of the guests began to arrive. Cassie and Mr. Ossory came first, then Mr. and Mrs. Dalton.

Selina presented her parents to the rest of the party a little anxiously, trying to judge them as the others might. Mr. Dalton was not as fashionable as the other gentlemen present, but he was dressed neatly and soberly, in keeping with his calling. He was a handsome gentleman of fifty, and it was obvious that Selina had inherited much of her good looks from him.

Mrs. Dalton was still an attractive woman at forty-five, but not as attractive as her hostess. Whereas Lady Kilbourne was thin and elegant, Mrs. Dalton was plump and motherly. However, both of her parents comported themselves with grace and dignity, and Selina was proud of them.

After tea, the party divided into smaller groups. Cassie and Mr. Ossory went with Malcolm to tour the stables. The Thistlewaites and Lady Kilbourne decided to rest in their rooms before dinner. Selina and her parents asked if they might go for a walk about the grounds, and Mr. Malcolm directed them to the parterre gardens on the south side of the house.

They walked in silence for a few minutes, arm in arm, Mrs. Dalton flanked by her husband and daughter. Selina, who had had an extra day to take in the magnificence of Hadley Hall, wondered if her parents were as overwhelmed as she had been the day before.

"So, Selina," Mr. Dalton finally said, "we were quite surprised to receive an invitation to Hadley Hall."

"I imagine you were," Selina said.

"Mr. Malcolm seems like a very nice young gentleman," Selina's mother said.

"Oh, Mama, do you like him? I am so glad," Selina said, turning a shining countenance toward her mother, who grabbed her hand and squeezed it, returning her daughter's smile.

"We have only had an hour's acquaintance with him, Millicent," Mr. Dalton said to his wife.

"And a very agreeable hour it was," his wife told him mischievously, looking remarkably like her daughter in that instant. Her husband smiled briefly at her and patted her other hand before becoming serious once again.

"Mr. Malcolm is everything that most parents would find pleasing: he is well-favored, wealthy, and well connected in society. But you know, Selina, your mother and I require more for you than that.

"You have been reared to prize virtue over wealth, and beauty of character over mere physical attractiveness. Mr. Malcolm is from a different sphere altogether. In his world, morality is laughed at, marriages are made for profit, and life is spent in idle, vain pursuits. Why, you have only to look at the activities of the Prince Regent and his brothers to see the truth of that."

"I know what you say is correct, Papa, but I think that by his interest in me, he demonstrates that he is different from his peers."

"That is true. You are not a nobleman's daughter, nor are you wealthy enough to make that a consideration. But you are a handsome young lady, and there have been many instances of physical attraction being mistaken for a more lasting emotion."

"Your father nearly fell victim to a siren's song at your age, my dear. If I had not been there to protect him, who knows what might have happened," said Mrs. Dalton.

"So you protected me, did you?" Mr. Dalton asked, his eyebrows raised.

"There is no need to thank me," Mrs. Dalton said.

Selina eyed her parents in amusement. It had always been thus. Her mother restrained her father from pontificating for too long, her humor keeping him from becoming too serious. It was a valuable quality in a clergyman's wife.

"I am so happy you both are here," Selina said.

"We are as well," Mrs. Dalton said. "Even if you and Mr. Malcolm should not make a match of it, it is so nice to have a little holiday."

Selina was relieved that evening to see that her father and Mr. Malcolm appeared to be getting on very well. The whole party, in fact, seemed to finally be in full swing. Julia was distracted from her previous bad humor by the arrival of Mr. Ossory, and Mrs. Thistlewaite was pleased to be able to retire to the background again with the influx of more guests. Lady Kilbourne and Mrs. Dalton discovered a mutual interest in gardening, and Cassie was always content when not wrangling with his cousin. (Which, with the advent of Mr. Ossory, was happening less and less frequently.)

The only thing to mar the high spirits of the party occurred after dinner, when the gentlemen rejoined the ladies in the drawing room. In the general conversation that followed, Mrs. Dalton turned to her daughter and said, "Oh, I forgot to ask you how Mrs. Covington is. Did you call on her as I asked?" Before Selina could reply, Mrs.

Dalton turned to her hostess and explained that Mrs. Covington was the widow of their cousin, and that she lived in town.

Selina's eyes flew to Malcolm, hoping against hope that he was involved in conversation and had missed her mother's remark. She was disappointed to find that he was staring right at her. Her next thought was that Julia might intervene, but Julia was speaking to her cousin and was oblivious to what was happening. Selina had no choice but to answer her mother.

"Yes, I did visit Mrs. Covington. She paid a visit to me at the Thistlewaites' town house as well."

"Good, I am glad to hear it." Mrs. Dalton turned again to Lady Kilbourne. "Mrs. Covington is not really a close connection, her husband was a second cousin only, but she is a widow. And Mr. Dalton and I have always taught Selina to show compassion to those in less fortunate circumstances."

Lady Kilbourne agreed that this was a good attitude to have, and the conversation soon turned to another subject. Selina, however, contributed very little to the discussion. She was completely embarrassed to have been caught lying by Mr. Malcolm, particularly when at practically the same moment her mother was praising her principled upbringing. She kept her eyes downcast, waiting impatiently for a time when she could excuse herself.

"Miss Dalton," she heard Mr. Malcolm say, and looking up, she saw that he had sat down in the chair on her left.

Selina quickly looked down again. "Mr. Malcolm," she said. "Pray excuse me, I am not feeling well—"

"Miss Dalton," Malcolm said again, cutting her off. "It does not matter to me that Mrs. Covington is your cousin, and I am sorry if I gave you that impression."

"She is not *actually* my cousin," Selina began, but then interrupted herself to say, "It is I who must apologize, Mr. Malcolm. I am so dreadfully embarrassed. What must you think of me?"

"I think that you must have been concerned for my good opinion and thought, if you told the truth, you would lose it. It is my fault, for I look back on that occasion with shame. I sounded dreadfully priggish, even arrogant, and I have heartily regretted it many times since."

"Even so, that was no excuse for me to *lie*. The only thing I can say in my defense is that I wanted to tell you the truth, but that Julia—" Selina paused, realizing it was not the thing to cast blame on someone else. "At any rate, I did want to tell you the truth."

"I believe you," Malcolm said. "Now, let's forget this foolish incident. It does neither of us good to harp on it."

Later that evening as Selina prepared for bed, she thought how pleased she was that her mother had introduced Mrs. Covington into the conversation, even though it had proved embarrassing initially. Her doubts about Mr. Malcolm's character had been based on Julia's statements about him and his disdainful remarks regarding Mrs. Covington. Now, after his apology, she no longer had any serious reservations about him. Julia's aversion to Mr. Malcolm was becoming more and more recognizable as wounded pride and could be dismissed, along with her spiteful comments. Mr. Malcolm had his faults like anyone else, but as far as Selina was concerned, he was close to perfect.

Selina's daydreaming was interrupted by a knock at the door. She wondered who could be coming to her chamber at this hour and was answered by Julia's head popping in from around the partially opened door.

"Selina, may I come in?" she asked.

Without waiting for a response, Julia closed the door carefully behind her and sat down on the window seat. "I think it is time," she said.

"If you think it is time for bed, I can only agree, and wonder why it is you're in my chamber instead of your own."

"No," Julia said impatiently, "I think it is time to show Mr. Malcolm your list."

"What list? I do not have a list."

"You know, we discussed all this before, when you first came to town. You are to allow Mr. Malcolm to find a list that you've written, except all the items will not be checked. Then he will see what it is like to be measured and found wanting."

"Julia, I know that Mr. Malcolm hurt your feelings and I am sorry for that. I believe you two started out on the wrong foot, and I think if you allowed yourself to get to know him—"

"Selina, what are you saying?"

"I am saying that I do not intend to take part in this . . . deception. I admire Mr. Malcolm. I do not want to hurt him."

Julia's eyes narrowed and she folded her arms across her chest. "So, now that you've seen Hadley Hall, seen how rich he is, you think you can get him to marry you, is that it?"

"No, that is not it! I am not interested in Mr. Malcolm because of his possessions. He has been very . . . kind to me."

"'He has been very . . . kind to me,'" Julia repeated, mimicking Selina. "Just wait till he spurns you like he did me, then you'll see how *kind* he can be."

"I don't believe he is like that." Selina sighed. "At least, I hope he's not."

"Well, this is all very touching, but it is not at all what was supposed to happen." Julia rose from the window seat to pace angrily about the room. "You agreed to help me."

"I agreed to think about it. Which I did. Very carefully. And I do not find Mr. Malcolm to be deserving of such a trick."

"And I? You think that *I* was deserving of such a trick?"

"No, but I do not think it was the same thing at all."

"But it was! It was exactly the same," Julia insisted.

"Mr. Malcolm did not set out to offend you. He had no way of knowing you would discover he had a list."

"But I did find out. He did offend me."

"And do you think you have never offended anyone? It happens, Julia. Frequently. A mature person accepts it and moves on. No one wants a person incapable of forgiveness for a friend."

"And I do not want a prosy preacher's daughter for a friend," Julia said, striding to the door.

"Julia," Selina said, but her only answer was the sound of a door being angrily closed.

Mr. Malcolm and his mother heard the sound from where they sat in the drawing room.

"What was that?" Lady Kilbourne asked.

"It sounded as if someone slammed a door."

"Probably that Miss Thistlewaite. She looks like the door-slamming type to me." There was a pause before Lady Kilbourne sighed. "Poor Mr. Ossory."

"Why do you say that?" Malcolm asked.

"She means to have him. And she's the type that gets her way." She looked up from her needlework for a moment to eye her son curiously. "What surprises me is that she did not set her cap for you. You are the more brilliant match."

"Oh, but she did. It was short-lived, however."

"What happened?"

Malcolm shrugged. "Nothing, really. I took her to the

opera once and then did not call again. It died a natural death."

"That is what you think. I doubt she'd forget a rejection like that very quickly. She is not enjoying taking second place to your Miss Dalton."

"She is not my Miss Dalton yet."

"Yes, I know," his mother said, somewhat wearily. "I wish you would hurry the business. You know how much I detest entertaining."

"So you approve of Miss Dalton?" Malcolm asked.

"Yes, of course. Although the more appropriate question is whether her father approves of us. Mr. Dalton is so very *worthy*. Really, if I had my wits about me, I would persuade you against marrying into such a family and allow you to marry some silly, ignorant girl by whom I would not suffer in comparison." Lady Kilbourne paused to take a sip of Madeira. "Someone like your sister-in-law."

"You would suffer no matter whom I married. You must realize that in-laws were designed by God to aid us in developing our character."

"I do realize it. And far be it from me to question the Almighty. Mr. Dalton would not approve."

10

Most of the party met again at breakfast the next day, the younger members dressed for riding, an appointment that had been made the previous evening. Selina eyed Julia a little warily, as they had not spoken since their last disastrous conversation, but Julia seemed in high spirits and looked very attractive in her military-style habit, which emphasized her fragile good looks. Selina felt it extremely unfair that Julia always managed to look so demure, when her personality was just the opposite.

Mr. Malcolm gestured to the empty seat next to his, so Selina chose something to eat from the sideboard and sat down.

"We were just discussing the ball we are planning to

hold next week," Malcolm told Selina. "Miss Thistlewaite would like it to be a masquerade. What is your opinion?"

Selina looked at her father, who was frowning slightly. She knew he did not have the best opinion of masquerades, considering them to be an excuse to indulge in all sorts of licentious behavior. "I have never been to a masquerade—" Selina began, but before she could finish, Julia had interrupted.

"See there, Mr. Malcolm, you must make it a masquerade. Selina has never been to one before."

"Would you enjoy that, Miss Dalton?" Malcolm asked her.

Selina hesitated, looking at her father. Mrs. Dalton whispered something in his ear and he smiled and shrugged his shoulders. "I suppose so," Selina said, unwilling to cross Julia when she seemed so pleased with the idea.

"Oh, wonderful!" Julia said, clapping her hands. Cassie looked less than pleased.

"I do not want to wear a costume. It's bound to be uncomfortable," he said, looking sulky.

"You can wear a domino," his cousin told him.

"That's even worse, dash it. Who wants to wear a cloak all evening? It's the middle of summer."

"As sorry as I am to have to miss the rest of this fascinating discussion, I must see to the horses," Mr. Malcolm said, getting up to leave. "Those of you who wish to ride this morning should join me at the stables when you have finished here."

After Mr. Malcolm left, Selina rose from her seat and joined her parents at the other side of the table. "Is the masquerade all right with you?" she asked Mr. Dalton, speaking quietly so the others could not hear.

"Well, you know how I feel about masquerade balls, but your mother reminded me that Mr. Malcolm is a trustworthy gentleman. I am confident he will not permit the sort of behavior that may attend these kinds of occasions in town."

"And it sounds like such fun," Mrs. Dalton said.

The group began their ride with Malcolm and Selina in the lead, followed by Julia flanked by Mr. Ossory and Cassie. However, after negotiating a narrow path, Selina found herself at Mr. Ossory's side, with Julia, Cassie, and Malcolm just ahead.

This was the first time they had been allowed a private conversation since their one drive together—Julia having been vigilant in keeping them apart—and Selina felt a little shy with him.

"So, it appears it is to be a chess match after all," he finally said, breaking the silence.

Selina was startled at first, but quickly grasped his meaning. "I am sorry, Mr. Ossory, it is just—"

"I know, I know. My friend has cut me out."

"I am so sorry," Selina repeated again, not knowing what else to say.

"Don't be sorry. It is entirely my fault. I arrived on the scene too late. I could have met you anytime the past three years if I had visited my aunt while on leave as she requested." Mr. Ossory paused, looking at Selina with a rueful grin. "To tell you the truth, I didn't have much confidence in Aunt Ossory's matchmaking ability. She had dreadful eyesight, you know."

"I do know. I was constantly keeping her from holding conversations with inanimate objects. She frequently confused her butler with the umbrella stand."

Mr. Ossory laughed. "Well, then, you understand my hesitation."

"I do indeed."

They rode in silence for a moment, Selina thinking what a shame it was that she could not love Henry Ossory, but then realizing if she were in love with him, she would not be free to fall in love with Mr. Malcolm, which was a dreadful thought. She realized if Mr. Ossory had visited his aunt a year or so ago, she probably would be married to him now. As much as she liked Mr. Ossory, she was glad he had not visited.

"It is not too late for us to be friends, however," Mr. Ossory said, interrupting Selina's tumultuous thoughts.

"No, it is not too late for that. I would like it very much indeed."

"Selina! Mr. Ossory!" Julia called.

Henry and Selina looked up to see that they had fallen behind the other riders, who had stopped to wait for them.

"Selina, this is not a drawing room," Julia said, in a playful tone of voice.

"I beg your pardon," Selina said, surprised that Julia was addressing her so kindly. Mr. Malcolm was frowning, but when he saw Selina looking at him he smiled at her.

"There is a very beautiful view from the top of that hill," Mr. Malcolm told them, pointing off in the distance. "Let us ride in that direction."

Later, as they were walking the horses back to Hadley Hall, Malcolm gestured to Julia and Henry, who were just ahead with Cassie.

"Do you think your friend Miss Thistlewaite will make a match with Mr. Ossory?" he asked Selina.

"Julia?" Selina asked, surprised. "I do not think Mr. Ossory is interested in her."

"I do not think so, either. I think he is interested in you."

Selina did not respond.

"Well?" Mr. Malcolm prompted her. "Is he interested in you?"

"It would be immodest of me to comment."

"That is the type of response I would expect from most women, but is not what I have come to expect from you."

"Mr. Ossory and I have agreed to engage in a match"— Selina paused for effect—"of chess."

Selina thought that Mr. Malcolm appeared relieved. She hoped so. She had been suddenly struck with the unworthy desire to make him jealous. "And had he a different match in mind?" Mr. Malcolm asked.

"Perhaps. But I told him I was only available for chess."

"Poor Henry," Malcolm said.

"Would you have preferred that I answer differently?" Selina asked, hoping to provoke him to something other than sympathy.

"I would have preferred that he go jump in the lake."

Selina was a little shocked she had achieved her ambition so easily, though she had definitely not wished for so rancorous a response. "That is an extreme attitude toward someone who is your friend," she said, looking at Mr. Malcolm in surprise. She was relieved to see that he was smiling.

"Oh, I do not really mean it. I only felt that way when he was making up to you. I knew he had a shared history with you, and I felt excluded. I was even jealous of your former employer. But now that I know him to have been unsuccessful in his pursuit, I no longer dislike him."

"I am relieved to hear it, for I like him very much."

"You had better not be too enthusiastic in your praise, or I might find myself despising him again," Mr. Malcolm said, but it was obvious he was joking.

"What, am I to like no one but you?" Selina asked.

"No, but you are to like me best."

Selina did not know how to reply to this, so said nothing. She couldn't very well tell him that she liked him better than any man she'd ever known.

At luncheon that day the conversation dwelt primarily on what costumes were to be worn to the masquerade ball. The gentlemen did not have much interest in the subject, but the ladies were quite excited, and even Selina began to think that it had been a good idea to hold a masquerade.

Lady Kilbourne suggested they look in the attics after luncheon. "For my sister never discarded a thing, and Jeremy put most of her belongings there after he inherited the house. There are probably costumes that could be contrived out of the clothing in the trunks up there."

"I don't need to go up to the attics," Cassie said, "although I will need to take a trip to the village to visit the dressmaker."

"Do you plan on going as a lady, Cassie?" Julia asked him.

"Of course not. A Greek," he said.

"Any particular Greek?" Mr. Ossory asked.

"No, though maybe I'd better come up with a name, in case someone asks. Perhaps Plato, or Socrates, or Julius Caesar."

"Julius Caesar was Roman," Selina told him.

"Roman, Greek, whatever you prefer. I just plan to wear a thin white robe and put some leaves over my ears. I went to one of these blasted things dressed as Henry VIII once and I almost suffocated."

"And what are you wearing, Selina?" Julia asked.

"I have no idea. I was hoping to receive inspiration when I visited the attic."

"Why not go as your namesake?" Mr. Malcolm suggested.

"My namesake?" Selina asked.

"Selene, goddess of the moon."

"Cassie has already stolen my costume," Selina said, smiling.

"I told you, I'm not going as a woman. I will be one of those philosophical fellows like Plato. Or Socrates," Cassie said.

"That is just about the most unlikely disguise I've ever heard of," Mr. Dalton said to Mrs. Dalton, who told him to be quiet.

Mr. Ossory and Mr. Dalton, who had already decided on their costumes, went to play billiards, while Julia, Selina, Mrs. Dalton, and Mr. Malcolm went up to the attic together. Lady Kilbourne retired to her chamber. She told her son she was too old to play dress-up, and would be wearing a ball gown to the masquerade.

After a bit of rummaging around, Mrs. Dalton found a gown from the previous century and decided to go as Marie Antoinette.

"I shall pretend I am seventeen again," Mrs. Dalton told Selina.

"Shall you powder your hair or wear a wig?" Selina asked her mother.

"A wig, of course. I am not like Lord Cassidy. I care nothing for comfort. It is how I look that is important," Mrs. Dalton said, laughing.

Having found her costume, Mrs. Dalton laid it aside and began to help the others search. Julia found a milkmaid's costume that had evidently been used for another masquerade years ago. "This is quaint," she said, holding it up before her.

"Oh, yes, my dear. You will look very charming in that," Mrs. Dalton agreed.

"So that leaves only Selina and Mr. Malcolm. Have you found anything, Selina?" Julia asked.

"No," Selina said. "But you all do not have to wait for me. I will continue looking on my own."

"Nonsense," Julia said. "We will help you."

Selina smiled and thanked Julia, relieved that she seemed to have forgiven her for refusing to take part in her scheme. She thought it strange that Julia still would not meet her eyes, but only murmured something and looked uncomfortable. Perhaps Julia had not completely forgiven her after all.

"So have you firmly decided against Selene, then?" Mr. Malcolm asked.

"No, not at all. I just thought if there was something ready-made I would use it, but I have no objection to masquerading as the moon goddess."

"I only ask because if you go as Selene, I intend to go as Endymion," Mr. Malcolm said.

"Who is Endymion?" Julia asked.

"He was the mortal love of Selene. Selene caught sight of him, fell in love, and begged Zeus to grant him immortality in the form of eternal slumber. According to the myth, Selene showers him with kisses every night as he sleeps on a hilltop," Mr. Malcolm explained.

"How romantic," Mrs. Dalton said.

"It is rather tragic if you ask me. What good does it do Selene to have an everlasting love when he is eternally asleep?" said Selina.

"I suppose she would rather have him sleep than die," Mr. Malcolm said.

"What does this moon goddess look like?" Julia asked.

Mr. Malcolm shrugged. "There have been some paintings, including one by Nicolas Poussin. In his painting Selene wears light, flowing garments and has dark hair. However, Homer said she had golden-colored hair. It has also been said that she was white of face and arms and that the moon reflected her glow."

"She wore a crescent moon on her head, too, I believe," Selina said.

"Well, that does not sound too difficult a costume. We will just have to make a shopping expedition," Mrs. Dalton said.

"What does Endymion wear?" Selina asked Malcolm.

"Actually, he's usually portrayed wearing nothing more than a judiciously placed piece of fabric, but that would not be appropriate for our ball," Mr. Malcolm said, grinning at Selina.

"Good heavens, no!" Mrs. Dalton exclaimed.

Selina said nothing. She was desperately trying to erase from her mind the image that his words had just created.

"So I will have great latitude in arranging my costume. I will carry a staff, so that everyone knows I am a shepherd, but other than that, I think it scarcely matters what I wear. As long as it's suitably rustic, of course."

Since there was no need to search for any more costumes, Mrs. Dalton and Julia collected theirs and started down the stairs. Selina remained behind for a moment with Mr. Malcolm.

"Is that why you wanted me to be Selene? So that you would have such an easy costume?" Selina asked him.

"I must confess I wanted us to have complementary costumes, but like Cassie, I did not want to be uncomfortable all evening, either. And I thought it fitting that Selina should go as Selene."

"So I am to arrange my costume so that you can be comfortable?" Selina asked, then sighed dramatically. "I have been grossly misled. I thought you were a romantic, and now I find that you are merely lazy."

"As befits my character, Endymion," Malcolm told her.

It took Selina a moment to understand him, and then she laughed. "You are not too sleepy, I see. You are quick-witted enough to offer excuses for your conduct."

They were interrupted by Mrs. Dalton calling Selina's name from where she was waiting below.

"I am coming, Mama," Selina called back, and she and Malcolm proceeded down the stairs.

For the next week everyone was busy making preparations for the upcoming ball. The ladies had volunteered to assist Lady Kilbourne in writing out the invitations, and when they were finished, Selina and Mr. Malcolm drove around the neighborhood delivering them. The ladies also took a trip to Tunbridge Wells, where they purchased the items that were not available at the nearby village.

Selina had found an illustration in a book titled *Costumes of the Ancients* in Hadley Hall's library and took it to the modiste. Her dress was to be white, with silver cording that crossed between her breasts and at her waist. She had thought at first that it would have been fun to dress a little more exotically, perhaps as a sultana or a Gypsy girl, but now she was becoming excited about masquerading as Selene. She was having a crescent moon headpiece made, and she had also found a picture of a coiffure in the same book.

Julia was very interested in Selina's preparations for her masquerade costume and insisted on helping her. Selina thought Julia was trying to make up for her previous behavior and thought it was rather sweet of her. She had no idea that Julia was making an exact copy of her costume.

For Julia had not given up on her plan to humiliate the Honorable Jeremy Malcolm. She had been indulged her entire life and taught to believe that she was superior to all others, and it had mortified her when she could not attract the notice of the prime catch on the marriage mart. Then, when Selina came and seemed to catch his notice so easily, she had been even further infuriated, even though she had planned for it to happen. What had disturbed her most was that Mr. Malcolm had liked Selina even without the stratagems Julia had believed to be necessary. Julia did not like feeling herself inferior to others, and she had hated playing second fiddle to Selina for the past few weeks. When Julia's new plan succeeded, Selina would be relegated back to second place, and Mr. Malcolm would learn what a mistake he had made in spurning her.

The only flaw in her plan that she could find was that Mr. Ossory seemed to admire Selina as well. If a match between Selina and Mr. Malcolm came to nothing, then it was entirely possible that Mr. Ossory would offer for Selina, a thought that greatly upset Julia. Julia wanted Mr. Ossory to admire *her*, even though she would obviously never marry him. He was a respectable match, to be sure, but he was not good enough for Julia Thistlewaite.

Though there were times Julia felt he was *too* good for her. His character was so noble, so open and honest, that when she was with him, it made her ashamed of the deception she was planning. However, Julia did not allow these rare pricks of conscience to deter her from her goal. Once set on a course of action, she was not the type to shrink back from carrying it to its conclusion, no matter what the consequences.

11

The night of the masquerade arrived and Selina eyed her appearance in the mirror with pleasure. Her dress was very flattering; the silver cording emphasizing her figure and the flowing white fabric rippling when she walked, giving the impression of moonlight. Her hair had been parted in the middle, then pulled back in a roll on each side, with two long braids falling over each shoulder. At the top of her head sat the silver crescent moon, and she had powdered her face and arms, then discreetly applied some rouge so she did not appear too pale.

Julia came into the room and looked Selina over from head to toe. Selina thought Julia looked very charming in her milkmaid's outfit, with its laced bodice and full skirt, and told her so.

"Thank you. You do as well," Julia replied, but she seemed distracted.

"Shall we go down?" Selina asked, and after she put on her mask, they left the room.

Mrs. Thistlewaite met them in the hall, and Selina wondered what it was she was supposed to portray. She was dressed in a black evening gown.

"And who are you this evening, ma'am?" Selina asked.

"I am a widow," Mrs. Thistlewaite said. "And you, Selina?"

"I am Selene, Greek goddess of the moon."

"So that is what the thing on your head is; I couldn't quite make it out. I hope it does not give you a headache," Mrs. Thistlewaite replied. Selina hoped that this would not be the general reaction to her costume.

The three ladies descended the stairs, meeting Mr. and Mrs. Dalton at the bottom.

"Selina," Mrs. Dalton said, before correcting herself. "Excuse me, *Selene*. You look wonderful. The costume turned out beautifully."

"Thank you, Mama. I am quite pleased with it. You look lovely too."

"Yes, well, at least she is not attired as a pagan goddess," Selina's father said.

"Thank you, Richard," Mrs. Dalton said, choosing to take his words as a compliment. He just rolled his eyes, but Selina was glad to see he was smiling.

She was beginning to understand her father's objection to masquerades. There was something very liberating about appearing under the guise of another. The very air around them seemed to pulse with excitement, and she felt as if anything could happen that night.

Selina and her parents walked through the various rooms, marveling at the changes to them. When she'd first arrived, she'd thought Hadley Hall was grander than anything she had ever seen, and tonight it surpassed even her initial impression. There were flowers intertwined around the pillars in the entrance hall, and satin hung on the walls of two of the rooms that adjoined the salon. Wax candles shone throughout the house, and each item had been cleaned and polished so that their light was reflected from every surface.

She entered the salon, which was being used for dancing, and was so distracted looking at her surroundings that she collided with another guest.

"I beg your pardon," she said, turning toward the person.

"It is I, a mere mortal, who should beg pardon from the illustrious Selene," the man said. It only took Selina a moment to recognize the figure as Mr. Malcolm, even though he was masked. He was wearing some sort of robe, fastened at one shoulder and belted at the middle. Selina noted with fascination that it left one shoulder completely bare, and hoped her father was not as shocked as she was. He was carrying a shepherd's staff and wearing sandals, and Selina thought that if Endymion really had looked like this, it would have been perfectly understandable that Selene had fallen desperately in love with him.

"You are pardoned," Selina said majestically once she'd recovered from her surprise.

"Then perhaps I might request the honor of this dance," Malcolm said, and after propping his staff against a wall, he led her onto the dance floor.

They were playing a waltz, and Selina was so relieved that she would be able to take part in it without humiliating herself as she had the last time that it took her a moment to realize that her hand was resting on his bare shoulder. She jerked her hand away, but Mr. Malcolm reached for it and placed it back on his shoulder.

"Surely the moon goddess is not frightened of a man of flesh and blood," Mr. Malcolm said.

"It is not your blood that frightens me," Selina said, and he laughed.

"You are forgetting that you are not Selina Dalton tonight," Mr. Malcolm said, pulling her a little closer.

"And you are forgetting that my parents are standing by that column, watching us," Selina said, putting the appropriate distance between them.

"I was trying to, at any rate," Mr. Malcolm replied irritably.

They waltzed in silence for a few minutes, and Selina began to feel sorry that she had destroyed the flirtatious mood between them.

"So, mortal, how are your sheep?" she asked.

"How are my sheep?" Mr. Malcolm repeated.

"Pardon me, but I am trying to pretend you are Endymion, and I do not know how to converse with a Greek shepherd boy."

"Forget that I am a Greek shepherd boy, and remember instead that we are lovers. How would you converse with me then?" Mr. Malcolm asked.

"I have as little experience with lovers as I do with Greek shepherd boys," Selina said.

"I am glad to hear it," Malcolm said, smiling. "But can't you pretend?"

"No," Selina said.

"I see it is up to me, then. My goddess, the moon cannot compete with your radiance this evening."

Selina was quiet a moment, before erupting into a nervous giggle.

"What is so amusing?" Malcolm asked her.

"I am sorry, but is that really how lovers speak to each other? It sounds like the most arrant nonsense. I do not think I can say that sort of thing with a straight face."

"How you can look the epitome of a seductive temptress and yet be so totally lacking in romance, I cannot understand," Mr. Malcolm said, shaking his head in mock disapproval.

"Do I look the epitome of a seductive temptress?" Selina asked, pleased by the remark. "No one has ever told me that before."

"Well, I should hope not. It is not a typical compliment in polite society."

"You look rather tempting yourself," Selina said shyly. "Seeing you tonight, I almost began to believe the myth."

"I thought you believed it to be a tragic story."

"I do. I meant the first part of the myth, where Selene falls so in love with the beautiful young shepherd that she requests he be given immortality. I would change the ending, so that he did not sleep through eternity."

"Well, I do not think he slept the entire time. He and Selene supposedly had fifty daughters together," Mr. Malcolm told Selina, and she could see the mischievous gleam in his eye even through his mask.

"It is just a story," Selina said.

"That is true. But for this one night, I want to believe it," Malcolm said.

Selina did not reply, and the rest of the dance was spent in silence, as Mr. Malcolm whirled her in dizzying circles around the dance floor. Selina did not waste her time thinking about a pair of fictional lovers, not when there was a very real man only inches away. She did not even notice Julia and Mr. Ossory waltzing nearby.

Julia had come down in her milkmaid costume and almost immediately encountered a dashing pirate from the previous century, though it took her a moment to realize it was

Henry Ossory. Henry was struck by how attractive the milkmaid was, and he, too, hesitated before tentatively identifying her. "Miss Thistlewaite?"

"Mr. Ossory?" Julia studied him for a moment. "I beg your pardon, but your costume seems completely out of character. Almost as much as Cassie's."

"I'm not sure how to take that remark. Do you find me dull and spiritless, not manly enough for swashbuckling adventures?"

Julia rushed to reassure him. "No, not at all. I think you're quite manly—" She stopped, embarrassed and uncharacteristically shy. "I mean . . . I can't imagine how we strayed onto this topic."

"It was my fault entirely, though I cannot regret the unintentional compliment you've given me. Would you care to dance?"

Julia and Henry joined the dancing, though both found themselves at a loss for words. Mr. Ossory was thinking that Miss Thistlewaite was perhaps not as bad as he'd previously imagined, and that she danced divinely, while Julia was attempting to behave as if she was unaffected by Mr. Ossory's touch, even though it was causing a nervous fluttering she'd never before experienced. So engrossed was she in these exhilarating sensations that she was shocked when her partner nodded toward Selina and Malcolm, breaking the silence to say to her: "It appears we'll soon be hearing wedding bells."

Julia, jolted from her tumultuous feelings by the sight of the other couple, quickly pulled herself from Mr. Ossory's arms as soon as the music ended.

"Thank you, I must go."

"Would you save the supper dance for me?" Mr. Ossory asked.

"Perhaps," Julia said, already walking away. Mr. Ossory watched her go, puzzled by her sudden change of mood.

When the music ended, Selina and Mr. Malcolm stood for a moment in each other's arms before walking from the floor as if in a trance. They were met by Julia, who effectively broke the spell by requesting that Selina come with her to her chamber. Selina reluctantly excused herself to Malcolm.

"When you return, I would like to dance again," Malcolm said. "Tonight we are in costume, so if we dance more than two dances no one is likely to know."

"I think everyone knows who *you* are," Selina said. "But I will dance with you at least once more," she promised before leaving the room with Julia. She was a little irritated with Julia for interrupting them. However, she was so happy she found she could not remain angry for long. She was sure that had been love shining in Malcolm's eyes as they danced together, and she began to wonder if he might propose to her that very night. If he did, she had no doubt what her answer would be.

"Why are we going to your room?" Selina asked, shaking herself out of her reverie as she and Julia started up the stairs.

"I need you to help me with my costume. I think that something has come undone."

"Have you seen Mr. Ossory?" Selina asked, sparing a thought for her friend's romance.

"Yes, we danced the last dance together."

"Did he like your costume?"

"I suppose so. He didn't really say," Julia replied, her resolve strengthening when she realized his only comment during the dance had been about Selina and Malcolm. When they reached Julia's bedchamber, she allowed Selina to precede her into the room, and then, remaining in the hallway, closed and locked the door behind Selina.

"Julia?" Selina called from the dark room. She did not at first suspect her friend of any evil intent, merely wondering why Julia had shut the door and left them in the dark. After repeated calls went unanswered and Selina tried the door and found it locked, she realized what had happened.

"Why, that little brat!" Selina exclaimed. She began to pound on the door, calling loudly for help. She did so for ten minutes or more without receiving a response. The music from the ballroom masked her cries, and all the servants were downstairs for the evening, waiting on the guests or working in the kitchens. She felt about for a tinderbox, and finding one on a nearby table, she lit a candle.

With the room lit, she saw another door that led to an adjoining chamber and tried that one. To her surprise, it opened. "Stupid girl," Selina said, walking through the other chamber and into the hallway. She could not wait to tell Julia what she thought of her immature prank.

Julia, in the meantime, went into her mother's room, where she had hidden the Selene costume earlier that evening. She hurriedly changed into it, putting on the wig she had fashioned into a copy of Selina's coiffure, and topping it with the crescent moon headpiece she had paid to have duplicated. She looked at her reflection in the mirror and thought she could pass for Selina in a room that was not too bright.

Julia could still hear Selina yelling for help as she left the room and went down the stairs. She would have to work quickly, just in case someone heard Selina. She approached a footman and handed him a slip of paper. "Please give this to Mr. Malcolm. It is urgent that he receives it immediately," she told him.

Then she walked quickly to the library, where she had requested in the note that Mr. Malcolm meet her.

She did not have long to wait. She had just been about to leave, having decided this was a very bad idea after all and that she should go release Selina, when Mr. Malcolm walked into the room.

"Miss Dalton. *Selina*," he said, and Julia was struck by the admiring expression on his face. When she compared it to the expression of near contempt he had always displayed in her presence, she began to feel that she was justified in her actions after all.

"This reminds me of our first meeting," Malcolm said. "Except I was the one holding a piece of paper in my hand."

He approached her where she stood in the darkest corner of the room. "Do you remember what you said to me?"

Julia shook her head.

"How could you forget so quickly? I remember every word we've ever exchanged. I told you that hope was a futile thing, and you disagreed with me. You said that you hoped I obtained what I was looking for. You had little idea it was *you* that I was searching for."

Mr. Malcolm paused and reached for her empty hand. "I wanted to wait, at least until the end of the house party, to be absolutely sure that I was making the right decision. But I do not think I can become any more convinced than I already am. Selina, would you do me the honor of becoming my wife?"

Julia could not believe how well Malcolm was fitting into her plans. "I am sorry, I cannot," she said, speaking in a whisper so as to disguise her voice.

"What?" Malcolm said, looking startled.

"I cannot marry you," Julia said.

"I do not understand. I thought you returned my feelings."

"I will not deny that I am fond of you, but I cannot marry you. You see, I have a list," Julia said, reminding herself to speak softly, even though she wanted to shout in triumph. She handed him the paper she was holding, and watched as he walked over to a brighter part of the room to read it.

She saw him scanning the list, which was titled "Qualifications for a Husband." All of the items had been checked off but one. She thought she could tell by his expression when he saw that item. It was: "Does not make others feel as if they cannot live up to an impossible standard."

When he finally looked up at her, an expression of shock and pain on his face, she turned and walked hurriedly from the room, ignoring his cry for her to wait.

Malcolm could not believe what he held in his hands. After years spent judging others, he could scarcely believe that *he* was the one who had been judged and found wanting. Someone, somewhere, was laughing at him, he was sure of it. He stood there a moment, defeated, looking at Selina's list in disbelief, before he realized that he would not allow it to end this way. He would convince Selina he *did* meet all the qualifications on her list, just as she met all the qualifications on his.

Selina ran hurriedly down the stairs and into the ball-room. She did not see Julia among the dozens of dancers, but she did run into Mr. Ossory.

"Miss Dalton, I thought you were in the library with Malcolm."

"What?" she asked him, still looking around for Julia.

"Well, perhaps I shouldn't mention it, but Malcolm received your note while he was speaking to me, so he told me about your appointment with him in the library."

"I made no appointment with Mr. Malcolm—" Selina started to say, and then stopped. She began to wonder if she should look for *Julia* in the library. She turned and left the ballroom, with Mr. Ossory following.

"Miss Dalton, is everything all right?" Mr. Ossory was saying as they approached the library door, when a woman in an exact replica of Selina's costume came running out of the library and into the hallway.

There was a shocked silence as Mr. Ossory looked from Selene to Selene. Then he said, "Miss Thistlewaite, is that you? What are you doing dressed like Miss Dalton?"

"Julia!" Selina said. "What is the meaning of this?"

Julia tried to edge past them, but Mr. Ossory detained her with his hand on her arm. "I think you had best explain what is going on, Miss Thistlewaite," he told her, his voice and expression stern.

"Selina," they heard Malcolm call from the library before he, too, joined them in the hall.

"What is this?" Malcolm asked, upon seeing the two Selenes.

"That is what we are waiting for Julia to explain," Selina told him.

"Julia?" he said, looking more closely at the second Selene. "Perhaps we should return to the library," Malcolm said.

They all filed into the library, Mr. Ossory leading a resigned Julia. Mr. Malcolm lit some more candles, removed his mask, and looked closely at Julia, who was seated next to Mr. Ossory on a sofa.

"So it was you who refused my offer just now, I presume," Malcolm said.

"What?" Selina exclaimed. "Julia, how could you?"

Julia, seeing three faces looking at her in strong disapproval, ripped off her mask and burst into tears.

"Well, Miss Thistlewaite?" Mr. Ossory said after a minute or two, apparently unaffected by her weeping.

"It is his own fault," Julia said, nodding her head in Malcolm's direction. "He spurned me publicly, all because I didn't meet a qualification on that rotten list of his. So I decided that he would know what it felt like to be judged and found wanting. I introduced him to Selina—"

"Selina! Don't tell me you played a part in this?" Malcolm asked.

"No, of course not," Selina said, but then her innate honesty came to the fore. "Well, that is to say, I did know about the list, but I did not want anything to do with Julia's little scheme."

"You knew about the list?" Mr. Malcolm asked.

"Yes, though you cannot think that I—" Selina said.

Malcolm interrupted her. "When did you find out about it?"

"The day I came to town Julia mentioned it to me, but you cannot think—"

"Would you please stop telling me what I can and cannot think?" Malcolm said, and Selina drew back in dismay. She had never seen Malcolm this way. Cold, unyielding, angry. "And would you please remove that blasted mask? The time for pretense is over."

Selina responded with dignity. "I have never pretended to be anyone other than who I am."

"So you did not lie to me and tell me that you were not related to Mrs. Covington?" Malcolm asked. "God, what a fool I've been. I should have seen it then," he said, running his hand through his hair.

"Jeremy," Selina said, crossing to where he was standing and placing her hand on his arm. "Please hear me out before you condemn me."

"And why should I believe you? It appears you have been deceiving me the entire time."

Selina shrank back from Malcolm as if she'd been

struck and collapsed into a nearby chair. Mr. Ossory felt compelled to stir himself in her defense. "Jeremy, perhaps you should listen to what Selina has to say."

"'Selina,' is it? It appears she has bewitched you as thoroughly as she has me. I do not think you are the appropriate person to counsel me. Now, if you would all excuse me, I am in the middle of giving a ball. A masquerade, ironically enough," he said, and left the room.

Selina sat as if turned to stone, and then a single tear ran down her cheek, tracing a path through the white face powder. Julia got up from the sofa and ran to kneel beside Selina's chair. "Selina, I am so sorry. Please say you will forgive me."

Selina ignored her, getting up from her chair and walking to the door. "Pray excuse me," she said, and left the room.

12

Julia was left facing a very angry Henry Ossory. "I hope that you are proud of your behavior this night," he said to her.

"Of course I am not. I feel absolutely dreadful. I feel like I'm going to be sick," Julia said, placing a hand on her stomach.

"Well, you should. You have completely ruined two people's lives, and for what? Some silly grudge you had against Malcolm."

"It was silly, was it not?" Julia said sadly. "It is odd—it felt very serious at the time."

Henry began to feel an inkling of sympathy for Julia. She made a very dismal picture, her nose red from crying, her hair mussed from the wig that had come off at some point during the heated discussion that had just taken place. In fact, Henry had never seen her look worse. She saw him looking at her and made a pathetic attempt to straighten her hair.

He smiled very slightly at her, which had the opposite effect for which it was intended. He was quite surprised when she threw herself, sobbing, against his chest. He began making soothing noises and patting her head, trying not to dwell on the fact that those Grecians didn't appear to wear much in the way of undergarments.

When her sobs dwindled to occasional hiccups, he began to wonder if it would be considered shabby if he pushed her away. The longer he held her, the more uncomfortable he became. He certainly did not want to be having lustful thoughts toward Julia Thistlewaite, of all people.

He was relieved when she finally drew away herself, apologizing for the wet spot she'd left on his coat.

"It is all right," he said, wondering if he could now take his leave of her. But she still stood, barely a foot away, her head tilted down, in a posture totally unlike the redoubtable Miss Thistlewaite, and he felt it would be rude to leave her in such a state.

"And I am sorry to involve you in all this as well. I imagine you and Selina will make a match of it now," she said, peeking up at him.

"Oh, I don't know," he said. "It may not be too late for her and Malcolm."

"But you admire Selina," Julia said. "Don't you want her to be free?"

"She will not be free if she is in love with someone else."

Julia sighed. "I wish I were more like Selina. Everyone likes Selina. It is quite infuriating," Julia said, sounding a little more like herself.

Henry decided that Julia would survive. "If you would excuse me, Miss Thistlewaite . . ."

"Oh, of course. You go ahead. I will just remain here and meditate on all my faults."

Henry walked to the door but turned back at Julia's voice. "Mr. Ossory, do you think Selina will ever forgive me?"

"I do not know," Henry said, his voice serious.

Julia nodded and put her chin up, furiously brushing away a tear.

Julia knocked softly on Selina's door. "Selina?" she called. There was no answer so she tried turning the knob, not too surprised to find that it was locked. She knocked again.

"Go away," she heard Selina say.

"Selina, please open the door."

"No."

"I will not go away until you open this door."

There was silence for a moment while Julia waited. Nothing happened, so she knocked again. Then the door quickly opened.

"There, the door is open. Now go away," Selina said, and shut it again.

"That is not what I meant and you know it," Julia said, turning the doorknob and finding it unlocked. She walked into the room and over to the window seat where Selina stared unseeingly out into the darkness.

Now that she was inside, Julia had no idea what to say. There was nothing she could do to excuse her actions; they were despicable. She stood there for a moment, wondering if she should leave, when Selina finally turned to look at her.

"If you are wondering whether or not you should lock me in the room, I assure you, I do not intend on going back down the rest of the evening. Feel free to masquerade as me until tomorrow if you choose."

"Of course I do not plan to lock you in your room," Julia said, but faltered under Selina's withering gaze. "Selina, I am so sorry. I cannot tell you how sorry I am."

"Do not bother. I do not want to hear it anyway," Selina said.

"You have every right to hate me. I hate myself. I should have listened to you weeks ago. But I was so jealous of you," Julia said.

"What are you talking about? You did this because you wanted to revenge yourself on Mr. Malcolm."

"I do not know why I did it. Initially I wanted to humiliate Mr. Malcolm, but later I wanted to ruin your chances with him as well. I could not bear that you were succeeding where I had failed."

"So now that you've destroyed my hopes of happiness with Mr. Malcolm, I imagine you're rather pleased with yourself."

"That's the strange thing about all of this; I am not the least bit pleased," Julia said.

Selina sighed. "I suppose it is not really important why you did it; it's too late to change matters now."

"Then you'll forgive me?"

"I'll do whatever you want if only you'll leave," Selina said.

"No, we have to figure out how to fix this," Julia said, dragging a footstool toward Selina and sitting down at Selina's feet.

Selina gave a little moan of exasperation and banged her head lightly against the window. "Why won't you leave me to dwell on my misery in peace?"

"Because I do not want you to be miserable. I want you to be happy," Julia said.

Selina studied Julia's earnest expression, and realized she sincerely meant what she said. "Then it seems as though we are both destined for disappointment," Selina replied.

"Mr. Malcolm loves you, Selina," Julia told her. "I should know. I was there for his proposal."

"If you want me to forgive you, you'd better not remind me of that," Selina said.

"My point is, if he loves you, he is sure to forgive you once he knows the whole truth. And that is what I plan to tell him."

"You forget that he believes us both to be liars and deceivers. He will not believe you are telling him the truth."

Julia looked perplexed for a moment, but then a look of triumph crossed her face. "Cassie," she said.

"What about Cassie?"

"Cassie will tell him. Mr. Malcolm will believe Cassie. And Cassie knows the entire story."

"You are actually suggesting that I entrust my future happiness to *Cassie*?" Selina asked.

"Yes, that is what I am suggesting, though I cannot believe it myself."

Selina shrugged, weary of the whole discussion. "I suppose I do not care if he tries, but I doubt he will succeed. I have never seen a man look so disgusted as Mr. Malcolm did this evening."

"He will get over it," Julia assured Selina. "He has to."

Julia left Selina and changed back into her milkmaid costume. She tried to repair her hair, but without her maid's help, whom she had already dismissed for the evening, she found it very difficult. She decided that milkmaids were probably not too fussy about their appearance anyway, and hurried back downstairs and into the ballroom to look for Cassie. She found him right away, standing against a pillar, watching the dancing. Even though it was not yet time for the unmasking, she would have recognized that long, lanky figure anywhere, even clothed in what looked like a bedsheet.

"Cassie," Julia said. "I need to speak with you."

"You know, Julia, I do not understand why you ladies complain so about having to wear dresses. This is quite a bit more comfortable than knee breeches, I can tell you. And when I walk there is the most refreshing breeze—"

"Cassie! I did not come here to discuss with you the advantages of feminine attire! I need to talk seriously to you about Mr. Malcolm and Selina."

"Ah. I see. You've finally caught on to the fact that your little scheme is useless. Well, I knew that all along. I could tell that Malcolm and Selina were perfectly suited for each other from the start. I imagine that stings a bit. You thought to humiliate Malcolm, and you end up presenting him with the perfect wife on a silver platter." Cassie chuckled a bit to himself, muttering, "And you wanted poetic justice."

"Well, Cassie, though it pains me to admit it, I have to concede that you were right about those two, and I was wrong. Furthermore, I have muddled things royally and I really need your help."

Cassie looked at Julia a little suspiciously, wondering if she was being sincere. He had never before heard words like that from his cousin's mouth. When he decided she was in earnest, his relaxed posture changed and his face took on an expression of resignation. "What did you do now?" he asked.

While the situation was being explained to Cassie by Julia, Mrs. Dalton approached them, asking if they'd seen Selina.

"I believe she is in her chamber," Julia said, looking highly uncomfortable.

Julia was sure by the searching glance Mrs. Dalton gave her that she suspected her of misbehavior, and was relieved when Mrs. Dalton just thanked her and left the room.

Mrs. Dalton did wonder why the Thistlewaite girl looked so self-conscious, and hoped she did not know something ominous about Selina. Mrs. Dalton had watched happily as her daughter danced the first waltz with her host, but shortly afterward her daughter had disappeared and Mr. Malcolm had come back into the ballroom with a look on his face that could curdle cream. He had then proceeded to dance with numerous sultanas and Gypsy girls, laughing and flirting in a manner that seemed totally at odds with his normal behavior of dignified restraint.

Mrs. Dalton, being a wise woman, could only conclude that he had quarreled with her daughter and, after waiting nearly an hour for Selina to reappear, decided to go looking for her. She had just begun her search when she chanced upon Julia and Cassie and, following their advice, went up to her daughter's room.

She knocked softly but, hearing no answer, opened the door and peeked in, calling Selina's name as she did so.

"What is it?" Mrs. Dalton heard her daughter say, although she could still not see Selina, as the bed draperies hid her from sight.

Mrs. Dalton walked into the room, closing the door behind her. "It is your mother, Selina," she said, walking toward her. Selina was huddled in a ball in the bed, and it was obvious she had been crying. "There, there," her mother said, sitting beside her and taking her into her arms, where Selina proceeded to cry violently while her mother rocked her, just as she used to do when Selina was a child.

Cassie was finally able to pull Malcolm aside in the Statue Gallery, which was being used as the refreshment room. He had waited impatiently for Malcolm to finish dancing, but it seemed his usually fastidious friend had picked this night to dance with every woman in the county, and it wasn't until one of Malcolm's partners requested refreshment that Cassie was able to get him alone for any length of time.

"Malcolm, I must talk to you," Cassie told his friend.

"You are talking to me," Malcolm said.

"No, I mean a serious conversation. Alone."

"I'm sorry, old friend, but this is a ball. No serious conversation is permitted at a ball. If you had wanted serious conversation, you should have gone to a dinner party, though I rather doubt you'd find any there, either," Malcolm said, picking up a glass and turning to leave the room.

"Malcolm, this is important. Please hear me out. It should only take ten minutes."

Malcolm turned to look back at his friend, whose usual easygoing expression had been replaced with one of resolve. He sighed, then nodded. "Let me take this to Miss Madison and then I will meet you in the library. Although I'd hoped not to return there this evening."

Cassie was sure his friend would relent toward Selina once he heard the entire story, but Malcolm seemed unmovable in his determination against the girl.

"I do not understand why you are telling me this," Malcolm said, after Cassie had finished his explanation.

"I am trying to make you understand it is not Miss Dalton's fault, it is Julia's. Miss Dalton was against the charade from the very start. Particularly after she met you, she again told Julia she did not want to become involved in her scheme. I think it would be obvious to you that Julia is the one who wished to humiliate you, not Miss Dalton."

"You have some nerve, pleading in Miss Dalton's behalf after the trick you conspired to play on me," Malcolm said, eyeing Cassie in a particularly unfriendly manner.

"I was *helping* you, if only you had the wit to see it. 'Tis true Julia's goal was to humiliate you. I, on the other hand, knew that Miss Dalton was perfect for you from the very start."

"Whether or not you believed you were helping me, the fact remains that Miss Dalton used information she had obtained from you about what I was seeking in a wife to become that woman. I do not even know her true character."

"That's not true! She barely paid any attention to what Julia and I were telling her. If she had listened to us, she probably would have not attracted your notice at all."

"So what you're saying is that she is even smarter than you and Julia."

"No! That is not what I am saying. That is, she is probably smarter than Julia and I, but . . ." Cassie ran a hand through his hair in agitation, knocking the leaves above his ears askew. "Dash it, you're twisting my words all around. What I am trying to say is that Selina Dalton is the right woman for you, Malcolm, and if you ruin this opportunity, you will regret it for the rest of your life."

"I appreciate your concern, but nowhere on my now infamous list does it specify deception, lying, or scheming. I am no longer interested in Miss Dalton, and can only regret that I ever fell victim to her little game."

Malcolm rose and walked to the door. "Please excuse me. I promised Miss Madison the next dance."

"I hope you trip and break your bloody stiff neck," Cassie mumbled.

"I heard that," Malcolm called back from just outside the door.

"Good!" Cassie replied.

Julia and Mr. Ossory had been waiting impatiently for Cassie to finish with Malcolm. When they saw Malcolm return to the ballroom, they quickly scurried to the library.

"Well?" Julia asked upon entering the room.

Cassie looked up, and Julia's hopeful air disappeared when she saw his expression. She threw herself rather ungracefully onto a sofa. "What happened?" she asked.

"He would not hear a word in Miss Dalton's defense. I told him the whole story, and now he believes Miss Dalton set out to entrap him."

"He does not deserve Selina," Julia said, but then her gaze fell upon Mr. Ossory, waiting to take Mr. Malcolm's place, and she quickly decided to herself that Selina would be better off with Mr. Malcolm.

"I do not understand why Jeremy is behaving so ungraciously," Mr. Ossory said.

"I was surprised myself. I've never known Malcolm to be so unfair," Cassie said. "Although there was that one time at Eton, when we were playing cricket—"

Julia cut ruthlessly into Cassie's reminiscing. "Perhaps he is still hurt," she said. "We are probably expecting him to recover too quickly. I am sure that tomorrow he will be more approachable. Once he has had time to think over what Cassie told him, he is sure to realize he is being unjust."

Mrs. Dalton was at that very moment telling Selina something similar. "My dear, things are bound to look better in the morning. From what you tell me, Mr. Malcolm has been grievously ill-used by those he thought he could trust. I am not referring to you, Selina," Mrs. Dalton hurried to say, when Selina looked as if she were about to protest. "I am referring to Lord Cassidy and Miss Thistlewaite. It cannot be a pleasant thing to discover that guests in your own home have been plotting and scheming behind your back. I am sure that once Mr. Malcolm recovers from his initial shock, he will soften toward you."

"Do you think so, Mama? Because I don't think I could bear it if he looked at me again the way he did tonight. Like I was some kind of vermin he'd turned up beneath a rock."

"I am sure you exaggerate. But even so, I do believe he will look at you differently in the morning."

But in the morning Malcolm was nowhere to be found. Selina reasoned he would sleep late after the late night he'd kept but, as she was unable to sleep herself, she was down early for breakfast. She was soon joined by Julia,

Henry, Cassie, and Mrs. Dalton, all of whom were very hungry or extremely slow eaters. They all dawdled at their breakfast until the clock struck eleven, and there was still no sign of Mr. Malcolm.

He finally made an appearance at luncheon, but he seemed more effectively masked than he had been the previous evening. He was polite to Selina but there was no longer any warmth in his gaze or tone when he addressed her.

She decided it would be best if she left Hadley Hall. It was clear that Mr. Malcolm had ceased to care for her. His expression now was so completely different from the look on his face when he had been in her company prior to last night's debacle that it was more than obvious any tender feelings he'd once entertained for her were gone.

"Mr. Malcolm, I would like to thank you and Lady Kilbourne for your kind hospitality, but I think it is time that my parents and I took our leave. We will be returning to Sussex in the morning," Selina said. She was surprised to see her mother shaking her head vigorously.

"I am sorry, Selina, I know we'd spoken of leaving, but I feel that I cannot leave yet. I woke up this morning with a tickle in my throat. I think I may be coming down with a cold." Ignoring her daughter's look of dismay, Mrs. Dalton turned to Mr. Malcolm. "I am afraid, sir, that we must trespass on your hospitality a little longer."

"It is no problem at all, Mrs. Dalton. Please stay as long as you would like. It makes no difference to me," Malcolm said politely enough, but his words stung Selina, who felt he was making plain his total indifference to her.

"Well, in that case, Mama, I may return with the Thistlewaites to town. I am sure they are eager to come home. Is it all right, ma'am, if I stay with you another week?" Selina asked Mrs. Thistlewaite.

"Why, of course—" Mrs. Thistlewaite was saying, only to be interrupted by her daughter.

"I am sorry, Selina, but Mama and I are not ready to return just yet. I find it so relaxing here in the country. I hate to return to the hustle and bustle of town."

Selina glared in frustration at her friend, thinking she had been overly hasty in granting her forgiveness last night. "Well. It seems that I will be staying a little longer at Hadley Hall after all," Selina said.

"I hope you enjoy the remainder of your stay," Mr. Malcolm said, although he had to know full well that Selina would not enjoy a single minute of it when he looked at her as if she were a stranger, and an unpleasant one at that.

"I think it is splendid that you are staying on, my dear," Lady Kilbourne said, and she at least sounded sincere. Selina turned to smile at her and was surprised to find Lady Kilbourne was regarding her with all the warmth that her son lacked.

13

Selina went to the library after luncheon, feeling that if she had to stay in this cursed house for a few days more she would spend the time reading in her room. That way she would be sure to avoid her host. She was disconcerted to find him already in the library.

"Oh, excuse me," she said, upon seeing him ensconced in a high-back chair by the empty grate. She turned to leave.

"There is no need to go. I assume you came to the library for something," he said, rising from his chair.

She stopped at the threshold, looking back at him over her shoulder. "I wanted a book, but I can come back later."

"You are here now. You might as well retrieve your book."

Selina walked to the bookshelves, but found it very difficult to focus on the titles, and the silence seemed to stretch on interminably. Selina thought Malcolm must have felt it awkward as well, as he cleared his throat before asking an innocuous question.

"So you enjoy reading, Miss Dalton?"

She stopped perusing the books to look at him. "I told you previously that I enjoy reading, if you recall."

"Ah, yes. I do recall that you said once that you enjoyed reading, but I have found that sometimes people will say things they do not really mean."

"I am not in the habit of doing so," Selina said. When he merely looked at her sardonically, she remembered that she had not told the truth about Gertie, and turned back to the bookshelf, blindly pulling a book from the shelves. She quickly turned to leave, but Malcolm stopped her by grabbing the book in her hand, turning it so that he could read the title.

"Poetry, Miss Dalton? A romantic, are you? I would have judged you a pragmatist," he said. She looked down at his hand, just inches from hers, linked by the book they both held.

Selina pulled the book from his grasp. "I am sure from now on I will be. I have recently learned that it is a mistake to hold romantic illusions. Reality has the habit of intruding, and it can be quite painful."

"I suppose by reality you mean truth. It is difficult to

hold on to our romantic illusions in the face of bitter truth, is it not?"

"Or in the face of what other people perceive the truth to be."

Malcolm merely smiled, and Selina was disappointed that the intensity had disappeared from his eyes, his face assuming the polite mask it had worn all afternoon. "You are very clever, I will give you that much," he said.

"Do you think so?" Selina asked. "I think I have been very stupid."

"Bravo," Malcolm said, clapping lightly. "You are playing the part of wounded lover very well indeed. Almost as well as your prior role."

Selina wanted to retort, but she found that her chest was very tight, and if she spoke she thought she might start weeping, which she refused to do in front of Mr. Malcolm. So she merely walked out of the room, leaving him standing there, alone.

By dinner that evening, Selina had decided the best thing to do would be to avoid speaking at all to Mr. Malcolm. Since he appeared to be ignoring her as well, this was not a difficult task.

The rest of the party tried to proceed as if there was nothing unusual occurring. Lady Kilbourne and Mrs. Dalton especially were making valiant efforts to carry the conversation, but it was obvious that there was a pall over the evening. Lady Kilbourne, Mrs. Thistlewaite, and Mr. and Mrs. Dalton played a desultory game of whist after dinner, but Mrs. Dalton was barely aware of what cards she was holding. Cassie, Julia, and Henry Ossory sat in one corner of the drawing room watching Selina pretend to read her book, while Malcolm wrote letters.

"We must do something," Julia whispered to her two cohorts.

"I think that is how this whole debacle began," Cassie said.

Julia started to respond but intercepted a warning glance from Mr. Ossory and so nobly decided to overlook her cousin's remark. "Mr. Ossory, what if you were to pay attention to Selina? I think Mr. Malcolm was jealous of you before. It may work again."

"I am not sure that would be a good idea," Henry demurred.

"Why didn't you ask *me* to spark Miss Dalton?" Cassie asked. "I'd be happy to."

"Don't be absurd. We are trying to make Malcolm jealous, not nauseous," Julia said dismissively, before turning to Henry again. "You would only have to pretend. And it should not be such a far stretch for you; you admitted that you admire her."

Henry couldn't explain why, but for some reason Julia's request made him angry. However, he reluctantly agreed to try, and approached Selina where she sat on the sofa, asking her loudly enough for Malcolm to overhear if she would like to take a walk in the gardens. He looked over at Julia for approval and wondered why, when he had only done as he was told, his reward was a fierce glare.

Since Henry was looking at Julia, he missed Malcolm's reaction to his request. Selina did not. She saw Malcolm look up from his writing with a slight frown, before looking down again when he noticed Selina watching him.

"I would be happy to walk with you, Mr. Ossory," Selina replied, in the same loud tone that Henry had used to make the request.

She was surprised when Henry looked somewhat disappointed at her acceptance, and then noticed him watching Julia, who also looked disappointed. "Perhaps Julia would like to come as well," Selina said, in a quieter tone of voice.

Both Henry and Julia brightened at the suggestion but Julia politely refused, and Henry and Selina set off on their walk.

There was a strained silence between them at first, the only sound the gravel crunching under their feet. Selina finally broke the silence to ask, "I thought we agreed to be friends, Mr. Ossory."

"What? Oh, of course," Henry said. "It's just—"

"It's just now that Mr. Malcolm is no longer interested in me you're afraid I may expect you to fulfill your aunt's expectation that we marry, is that it?"

"Well, yes, and I would not have minded a bit a week ago, but now . . ."

"Now you find yourself attracted to Julia?" Selina offered when Henry seemed unable to complete his sentence.

"No, not at all!" Henry said. "Well, perhaps just a little, but that is not to say that I will marry her. Though I am not saying I would not marry her."

Selina laughed. "Well, as long as you are clear on the subject."

Henry smiled ruefully. "I sound like an idiot, don't I? I really don't understand it myself. I didn't even like Miss Thistlewaite a week ago." He sounded genuinely confused, and Selina laughed again.

"I think that her association with you is bringing her better qualities to the fore," she told him.

"I hope so. I must say, I was completely appalled by her behavior last night. But I believe she sincerely regrets it."

"I agree. And I cannot blame her too much, because it has revealed to me who Mr. Malcolm *truly* is. I now think that Julia may have been more correct in her reading of his character than I was."

Henry shook his head. "I am sorry to contradict you, Miss Dalton, but I believe you are wrong. Miss Thistlewaite's actions were prompted by selfishness and pride. She never truly *wanted* to know Malcolm. I think you had come to know the real Malcolm. And I think his behavior now is in reaction to the tremendous wound he received."

"Yes, the wound to his pride," Selina said.

"Perhaps his pride was wounded, but I think that it

goes deeper than that. He was prepared to marry you. That must illustrate the depth of his attachment."

Selina sighed. "I thought so, at first, but the way he looks at me, the way he speaks to me!"

"It has only been one day. Give him time."

"I don't really have a choice, do I? My mother and Julia have hampered my efforts to leave."

"They are only looking out for your best interests."

"And is that why you're out walking with me as well?" Selina asked.

"Well, to tell the truth, Miss Thistlewaite suggested it. She thought it might make Malcolm jealous if I showed you some attention. But I am very pleased to walk with you."

"But you'd rather be walking with Julia." Selina stopped him when he would have protested. "It is perfectly all right. I must admit if I had my choice I would prefer to be walking with Mr. Malcolm. If he did not despise me, that is."

"If it's any consolation, Cassie was very willing to walk out with you, but Miss Thistlewaite did not feel that would have the desired effect."

"Not to mention that my toes would be in danger the entire time."

Selina and Henry returned to the drawing room in obviously higher spirits. This had the unusual effect of depressing at least two other members of the party. It caused Mrs. Dalton, however, to begin looking Mr. Ossory over more carefully. Selina saw the direction of her mother's gaze and realized she needed to speak with her. She did not want her mother thinking that if Mr. Malcolm did not come up to scratch, Mr. Ossory would make a satisfactory replacement.

14

*T*he following morning passed in much the same manner, with Malcolm and Selina politely ignoring each other. Selina returned to her room after luncheon to find a note had been delivered there. She told herself not to become excited over nothing, although her first thought upon seeing the note was that it was from Mr. Malcolm. When she opened it, she found it was an invitation from her hostess to tour the conservatory at two o'clock. Selina was to meet Lady Kilbourne and the rest of the party there.

A servant directed Selina to the conservatory and left her at the entrance. When she opened the door, she was immediately hit with a gush of warm, scented air. Selina looked around her in amazement at the variety of exotic plants and trees, many of which were blooming, and most of which she had never before seen. She began to walk slowly down the first aisle before eventually ending up in the middle of the conservatory, which had a high, pointed ceiling made of glass.

She had just begun a tour of that area as well when she was startled by the sound of someone clearing his throat. Looking up, she saw Malcolm standing by one of the stone benches that formed a circle in the middle of the room.

"I suppose I have you to thank for this," he said, holding out a slip of paper.

"I beg your pardon?" Selina said.

"If you thought to entrap me by arranging a compromising situation, I must say I had believed you a great deal cleverer than this. If anyone found us alone together, it is hardly a situation that would warrant a marriage proposal. Or perhaps you planned to throw yourself into my arms when given a signal by your accomplice. Who is it, by the way? Miss Thistlewaite?"

"I have no idea what you are talking about," Selina said. "I received an invitation to meet at two o'clock at the conservatory for a tour. I assumed it would be a group tour. I certainly did not plan on meeting you here."

"And I suppose it is a coincidence that I received a note as well. However, mine did not mention anything as innocuous as a tour. Mine spouted some nonsense about 'a discussion that will promise great future benefit.' It was quite gothic, now that I think on it."

"Then I am surprised you bothered to come," Selina said.

Malcolm shrugged. "My curiosity was piqued."

"Well, if you are so frightened of my treacherous schemes, why don't you just leave?"

"I will," Malcolm said, but made no move to do so.

"I am glad to hear it."

"Are you remaining here?" he asked.

"No, I shall leave as well," Selina said. "The conservatory has lost most of its charm for me." She flounced off, walking back the way she came, traversing the distance much more quickly than she had earlier. She grasped the handle to open the door and it refused to open. She pulled again but it still remained closed.

Malcolm was standing directly behind her. "Well? Did you change your mind?"

Selina pulled again, rather desperately, but the door still did not budge. "The door appears to be stuck," she said. "It must be the humidity."

"Let me try," Malcolm said impatiently, reaching for the handle. He, too, could not open the door. "It is certainly stuck, but I rather doubt it is the humidity," he said, turning to look at Selina, his arms folded across his chest.

"What do you think it could be?" she asked, before realizing he was accusing her again of attempting to ensnare him. "You—you arrogant, conceited coxcomb! I would rather marry the gardener!"

"I will be sure to inform Thompson of your regard," Malcolm said.

Selina did not reply, but walked regally back to the stone benches and sat.

"What are you doing?" Malcolm asked, following her.

"I am waiting for whoever locked us in to return, and I'd rather do so sitting, if you don't mind."

"Is there a certain time they are scheduled to return?" Malcolm asked, dropping down onto a bench opposite Selina.

"For the last time, would you please rid yourself of the notion that I had something to do with our predicament? I do not enjoy being forcibly confined, and I am growing rather tired of the experience."

"I am afraid I do not understand. Have you been incarcerated in the past for a crime?"

"Of course not. Julia locked me in her room the night of the masquerade so that she could pose as me. If I find she is behind this as well, I will not be so quick to forgive her a second time."

"I must say, you do seem to have rather unfortunate taste in friends."

"So I have recently discovered," Selina replied, with a significant glance at Malcolm.

Her remark seemed to have made a small dent in his reserve, for his face took on a startled, conscious look that he quickly hid by coughing into his hand. They both sat there quietly for a few minutes, Malcolm casting several quizzical glances at Selina.

"Well, if we are to be cooped up here for a while, we may as well converse. So why don't you tell me about yourself, Miss Dalton."

"I believe you asked me something similar at the beginning of our acquaintance, and I told you such a blatant request was unlikely to be fulfilled."

"Yes, I remember. No doubt you were trying to conceal your background at the time."

Selina gave an exasperated sigh, and then began retelling the events of her life in a singsong fashion. "I was born in Chailey, Sussex, on March 28, 1796. My father served as vicar, and his living was supplied to him by a relation of his, Lord Musgrove. I have five younger brothers and sisters, though one of my brothers, Charles, died from typhus fever when he was three. I attended Mrs. Finch's Lady's Academy from the ages of fourteen to seventeen, where I made the acquaintance of Julia Thistlewaite. At the age of eighteen, I accepted a position serving as companion to Mrs. Ossory of Bath. She died a few months ago, after which I accepted an invitation from Julia to come to London. While in London, I made the acquaintance of a gentleman who invited me and my family to his estate in Kent, apparently for the sole purpose of tormenting me."

Malcolm continued to eye Selina suspiciously. "You

sound as if you are repeating what someone instructed you to say," he said.

Selina restrained herself from screaming in exasperation. "I am done speaking with you," she told Malcolm. "We can sit here in silence for the next fortnight, for all I care."

"I am sure we will not be locked in here for a fortnight," Malcolm said, but Selina maintained her stony silence.

She was not sure how long they sat that way—Malcolm casually sprawled on his stone bench, Selina sitting upright and tensely upon hers—when she became acutely aware of how very hot it was. There were beads of sweat trickling down her neck and back, and her dress was sticking to her. She looked over at Mr. Malcolm, who also appeared to be suffering from the heat. His cheeks were flushed and he, too, looked to be perspiring.

"I had determined not to remove any clothing, for fear of how that might be construed, but I am afraid I must remove my jacket if I am to remain conscious," Malcolm said, breaking the long silence. "Do I have your permission?"

Selina inclined her head slightly, determined not to break her vow of silence. She watched as Malcolm shrugged out of his tight-fitting jacket, and then his waistcoat, his linen shirt almost transparent underneath, he was so wet from perspiration. He removed his cravat as well, and she watched in fascination as a trickle of sweat slowly traced a path down his neck to finally disappear under his shirt collar. She was suddenly hotter than ever, and raised her hand to fan herself.

He appeared to be studying her with equal deliberation, and Selina looked down to find that her thin muslin dress had become literally soaked with sweat. She hoped it had also not become as transparent as Malcolm's shirt. She could not remove any clothing to make herself more comfortable—she was not wearing a spencer—but she did remove her gloves, sighing with relief as she did so.

She was surprised when Malcolm shot up from the bench across from her and began pacing. She thought it was much too hot for such exertion, although she watched him languorously, finding that it was too hot for her to remain angry as well. She would rather think about how beautiful he was, one dark lock having fallen across his forehead, his tall, lithe figure displayed to advantage in his shirt and pantaloons. He stopped pacing all of a sudden, approaching her where she sat on the bench.

"You do not look comfortable, Miss Dalton," he said, his voice a little raspier than usual. He cleared his throat. "Are you suffering from the heat, perchance?"

Selina forgot her vow of silence. "It is most dreadfully hot," she whispered.

"There is a fountain about here somewhere," he told her. "Perhaps if we were to rest our feet in the water it would have a cooling effect on the rest of our—that is, it would cool us down."

Selina nodded, and followed him to another part of the conservatory, where a shallow granite fountain bubbled noisily. It was a large circular fountain, and was the center-piece of the room in which they found themselves. Selina felt that she had never seen such a beautiful sight, and wished for Malcolm to be gone so she could bathe more than just her feet. He was not, however, so she sat on the edge of the fountain and removed her shoes. She turned to find that he was doing the same, but wondered how she was to remove her stockings with him present. He fin-ished his endeavors and noticed her looking at him.

"I will turn my back so you can feel free to remove your stockings," he told her, turning away. She quickly removed her stockings and called out to him when she had finished. He had rolled his pantaloons up to his knees and Selina hurriedly looked away from the sight. There was something altogether too intimate about them being alone together with bare feet and legs. She turned back to the fountain, pulling her dress up around her knees and stepping in before sitting down on the narrow ledge.

The water was not as cold as Selina might like, but it felt like heaven to her overheated skin. Malcolm must have felt similarly, because he let out a contented sigh.

Selina reached down tentatively with one hand and rubbed some of the water on her bare arms. She was sur-prised when Malcolm appeared suddenly at her side, hold-ing a wet handkerchief.

"If I may," he said, holding it toward her. She nodded,

and he placed the handkerchief on her face, tenderly wiping it.

"That feels wonderful," Selina said, her eyes closed. She opened them quickly when the handkerchief traveled down her neck. Malcolm stopped, his hand resting at the base of her throat, and they sat like that for a moment, which seemed like an eternity, looking at each other, their breathing almost as loud as the fountain. Then somehow they were in each other's arms.

Selina could not remember later how it happened—if he were the one to make the first motion toward her or if she were the one to throw herself upon his chest. It was too hot, too hazy to think clearly, and she only knew that she was right where she wanted to be. She wasn't sure, either, how they ended up in the water. She thought in the beginning they were both sitting on the edge of the fountain, their feet still in the water, but at some point she found herself submerged in the shallow water, with Malcolm beside her, passionately kissing her.

It was in this state that the rest of the house party found them.

The sound of voices had just begun to register on Selina's consciousness, when she heard her name spoken loudly. Still entangled with Malcolm in the shallow fountain, she looked up to see Mrs. Dalton staring at her in horror.

"Mama," she said, and closed her eyes, thinking perhaps when she opened them this would prove to be an illusion brought on by the heat. She opened them to find it was no illusion, and that her mother was still there.

Malcolm roused himself to action, disentangling himself from Selina and nearly drowning her in the process. "Madam, I assure you, this is not what it seems," he told Mrs. Dalton, sitting upright in the shallow pool.

Selina raised herself up as well, trying to wipe the water from her eyes. When she was finally able to see again, she realized Julia was looking at her in horror while most of the gentlemen were averting their gaze. Selina quickly looked down at herself, before plopping back into the water. Her dress was clinging to her in a most embarrassing way, and she had no desire to parade before the house party in such a state.

She was thankful when Lady Kilbourne called for a servant and sent for some towels, before approaching Selina and Malcolm where they sat in the fountain. "Tell me, Jeremy, if this is not what it seems, what is it, exactly?"

"Miss Dalton and I were cruelly locked in the conservatory, which became dangerously warm. Fearing for our safety, we took refuge in this fountain," Malcolm said, quite seriously, before coming to a stop and sighing. "Miss Dalton and I would like to announce our engagement," he said in resigned tones.

"Splendid," Lady Kilbourne said. "That is exactly what it seemed." Lady Kilbourne turned away from Selina and Malcolm to address the others. "I think that I should remain behind with Malcolm and Miss Dalton while the rest of you continue your tour of the conservatory. You really must see the orangery," Lady Kilbourne told her guests, literally pushing Cassie in that direction when he seemed inclined to linger by the fountain, gaping at Selina.

Selina found herself shivering, hardly able to believe that only a short while ago she had been overly warm. Now, completely embarrassed and acutely aware of the sordid appearance she presented, she wanted nothing more than to disappear. She put her knees in front of her, clasped them against her chest, and rested her head on top of them, still sitting in the shallow water. Malcolm made no move to leave the fountain, either, although he had managed to put a great deal of space between himself and Selina.

Lady Kilbourne, having seen her guests on their way, turned back to look at Selina and Malcolm, each sitting disconsolately on either side of the fountain, soaking wet.

"I do understand why you might entertain a certain fondness for that fountain, but do you plan on remaining there the rest of the day?" she asked them.

Selina opened her mouth to speak, but fell silent when Malcolm said, "We are waiting for the towels."

"Yes, I suppose you are. It might prove rather embarrassing for you to come out now, in all your glory. Ah, it looks like the towels have arrived."

Selina thankfully accepted a towel from a footman, trying to ignore the look of curiosity he was unable to restrain. She supposed her escapade would be a topic of much discussion in the servants' hall that evening. She held the towel in front of her like a shield while she rose before wrapping it around her. Stepping out of the fountain, she reached for her shoes and stockings, and then turned, preparing to run to her chamber.

"Miss Dalton," Lady Kilbourne said, stopping her. "Surely you do not intend to leave without even a farewell to Jeremy? Or perhaps you wish for some privacy? I am sure that is perfectly understandable now that you are a newly engaged couple. Just do not begin cavorting about in the fountain again. I am not sure how many clean towels there are."

"Mother," Malcolm said. "I am sure I can speak for Miss Dalton when I say all that we desire is the privacy of our bedchamber." When his mother didn't answer, but merely raised her eyebrows, he realized that his statement did not come out as he'd intended. "Our respective bedchambers, I mean to say. We need to get out of these wet things before we catch our death. There will be plenty of time for us to talk later."

Selina looked over at Malcolm, and was not surprised to find him looking at her if he would like to murder her. *He probably thinks I planned this entire thing,* Selina thought before excusing herself to Lady Kilbourne and running to her room.

15

$\mathcal{S}$ elina had planned on changing her dress without assistance, thereby avoiding the curiosity of Mary, the maidservant who had been assigned to her during her stay at Hadley Hall. It seemed, however, that word of Selina's disaster had already traveled to Mary, for she was waiting in Selina's room when she arrived and had ordered a bath. Mary said nothing, but Selina's humiliation was complete when Mary pulled a piece of vegetation, most likely a water lily, from her chemise.

She was bathed, mostly dry, and clothed when her mother came to her room just as Mary was leaving. "Selina, my dear, what happened?" Mrs. Dalton asked her as soon as the door had closed behind the maid: Selina was sure Mary was regretting that she hadn't made an excuse to linger.

"Oh, Mama, I have never been so embarrassed in my life," Selina cried, hiding her face in her hands.

"Yes, I realize that, but is it true you are engaged to Mr. Malcolm?" It was obvious Mrs. Dalton considered that the more important of the afternoon's events.

"If I am, I do not want to be. I know that he believes I engineered the entire thing. As if I would want to be observed thus by my family and nearly all of my acquaintances. I do not think I can face any of them again."

"Well, I must admit I was rather startled to see you in so intimate an embrace with Mr. Malcolm, but if he is willing to marry you, then it will make everything right. But of course there was no question whether he would do the honorable thing. It would be unthinkable of him to refuse. Your reputation would be in tatters."

"Mama, I do not find this kind of talk very encouraging," Selina said.

Her mother merely patted her hand, before asking, "Selina, how did you come to be in a *fountain*, of all places?"

"It was so very hot, it seemed a good idea at the time. Oh, I don't know!" Selina wailed, throwing herself on the bed and burying her face in a pillow. "Please give my excuses at dinner," she said, her voice muffled.

"Nonsense. You are engaged to the Honorable Jeremy Malcolm of Hadley Hall, Kent. Where he chooses to embrace you is no one's affair. There is no need to hide your head in a pillow. I think you should come down to tea."

"I definitely am not coming to tea," Selina said before being interrupted by a knock at the door.

"Yes?" Selina called.

Mary opened the door a crack, sticking her head in the room. "Mr. Malcolm requests your presence in the library, miss."

"Tell him I have caught a horrible chill—" Selina said, but her mother's voice overrode hers.

"Tell him she will be down momentarily," Mrs. Dalton said authoritatively.

"Yes, ma'am," Mary said, dropping a curtsy before shutting the door.

Selina paused at the threshold of the library, observing Malcolm as he stood before the window. His hair, like her own, was still damp, and she found the sight both embarrassing and exciting at the same time. *Why can this not be a real engagement*, she thought as she stared at his handsome profile. *Why does he have to believe so ill of me?* He turned then, and saw her standing in the doorway.

Malcolm's thoughts upon seeing Selina were just as tumultuous. He could not believe he had fallen into her trap so easily, and it angered him that he had been so vulnerable. His extreme caution had always protected him from being caught in any kind of compromising situation, no matter the temptation. But he was finding Selina extremely hard to resist. Even now, as she stood there, hesitant to come into the room, her big green eyes displaying her trepidation, he found himself wanting to finish what they'd started in the conservatory. And as much as he hated being trapped into marriage, another part of him rejoiced at the thought that once they were married, he would have every right to continue his exploration of her lips, of that beautiful body . . .

He shook his head to clear it of such thoughts and tried to revive his anger at her for playing so devious a trick on him.

"Miss Dalton, please come in," he told her. Selina barely suppressed a sigh. He still, even after being observed intimately embracing her in a fountain and publicly announcing their betrothal, persisted in calling her Miss Dalton.

"I have spoken to your father, and he has consented to our engagement. So we should discuss when and where you would like to hold the ceremony. I assume you would like to be married in your father's church?"

"You mean to go through with this?" Selina asked.

"Of course. I cannot in honor do anything else. You have been hopelessly compromised and, as a gentleman, I must redeem your reputation." He smiled wryly. "You are to be congratulated, Miss Dalton. I have avoided many attempts to entrap me into marriage, but never have I met someone with methods as original as yours."

"So you believe I planned the events of this afternoon?"

"I do not believe them to have been an accident. It is too coincidental that we would have been locked in the conservatory and then the entire party of guests would have felt compelled to tour that same conservatory exactly one hour later, observing us in a compromising position."

"And I suppose I am to be blamed for the *position* we were found in as well?" Selina asked, looking directly into Malcolm's eyes. She was pleased to see Malcolm's gaze drop at her question.

"No, I must admit you are not entirely to blame. If I had been stronger, the entire incident could have been avoided. But I have never denied that I find you . . . extremely attractive, and I am just a man, after all," Malcolm said, his eyes on Selina's wet hair. His voice had lowered quite a bit, and Selina knew he was thinking of the passionate embrace they'd shared before they were discovered. She spoke up quickly before she found herself caught in a similar situation again. The look in his eyes was positively scorching.

"So I am expected to marry a man who will resent me the rest of his life for forcing an unwanted marriage on him?"

"I would of course be obliged to overlook your unfortunate past if we are to be comfortable together," Malcolm said. Selina told herself she was happy to see that Malcolm no longer had lovemaking on his mind. His manner had returned to its previous rigid formality.

"How generous of you. And I suppose I would then be forced to assume an attitude of humble gratitude toward you for your forbearance."

Malcolm shrugged. "You may assume whatever attitude you please, as long as there is a modicum of politeness and civility between us."

"Politeness? Civility? *This* is what you desire in a marriage?" Selina asked, her voice beginning to rise.

"It is true that I had originally hoped for more, but due to the unfortunate circumstances of our betrothal, I know I must content myself with less."

"Well, I know no such thing. I will not content myself with marriage to a man who holds such a low opinion of me. A man who believes I conspired to entrap him, and would never let me forget it for the rest of our lives together. I thank you, sir, for your *kind* offer, but I am afraid I must refuse."

"Come, Selina, you know you cannot refuse. Too many people observed us this afternoon. Your reputation would never recover."

Selina was too upset to notice his use of her first name. "I do not care if all of England observed us this afternoon, I would still not marry you. It was just a kiss, for heaven's sake."

Malcolm raised his eyebrows at the dismissive way she referred to their embrace and murmured, "*Just* a kiss?" But Selina ignored his remark, still infuriated.

"You, sir, are the most insufferably arrogant man it has ever been my misfortune to know. I thought Julia was very wrong in her scheme to humble you, but now I find myself wishing I had taken a more active part! Although when I think on it, I realize her plan would never have worked—it was flawed from the beginning. She expected you to fall in love with me, you see. I have since learned that you are incapable of forming such an attachment. You are too in love with yourself!"

Selina turned and ran from the library, ignoring Malcolm's requests for her to wait. He was left standing in the middle of the room.

"Damn and blast," he said, just as his mother entered.

"You do not sound like a man who has just become happily engaged," she observed.

"That is because I am *not* happily engaged. Indeed, I am not engaged at all. Miss Dalton has categorically refused me."

Lady Kilbourne sighed. "You have ruined things, haven't you, Jeremy? And after all my efforts. It was a very warm afternoon to arrange a tour of the conservatory."

It took a moment for Malcolm to comprehend what his mother was saying, as he was still brooding over his conversation with Selina. Lady Kilbourne waited patiently until he grasped her meaning. When he finally did, his head shot up and he focused his complete attention on her. "What did you just say?"

"I am saying that I arranged for a tour of the conservatory. At three o'clock. I assumed that would give the two of you enough time alone to come to some sort of an agreement. However, even I was surprised to find you splashing around in the fountain together. I rather think that's the sort of thing a parent does not really wish to see," Lady Kilbourne said thoughtfully. "I think the good vicar was even more shocked than I."

Malcolm was still staring, his jaw hanging open in disbelief. "Are you telling me that *you* arranged the events of this afternoon?"

Lady Kilbourne shook her head sadly. "I have already told you so. Twice, I believe."

"Why did you not tell me this earlier?"

"I thought I'd give you a chance to clean up. If I'd known you were in such a great hurry to bungle things, you can be assured I would not have exercised such forbearance."

Malcolm did not reply, but walked to the window to stare out unseeingly at the lawn. His mother watched him for a moment before asking what it was he'd done to upset Selina.

"Oh, nothing too serious. I merely accused her of arranging our incarceration in the conservatory so that she could entrap me into marriage."

Lady Kilbourne sighed heavily. "I might have known. Mrs. Dalton told me you'd already accused Selina of playing a part in Julia Thistlewaite's little scheme."

"Now, *that* was not an unjust accusation. I did catch her out in a lie."

"Probably at Julia's instigation. It is obvious *she* would have no compunction in using Selina to achieve her own ends. I must say, Jeremy, I am quite disappointed in you,"

Lady Kilbourne said, looking at him with an expression that made him feel six years old. When he would have spoken, Lady Kilbourne held up a hand, motioning him to silence. "Hear me out, please. I am well aware that you have a list. I have been aware of it for some time. I was pleased that you were taking the matter of matrimony so seriously and even wished your brother Robert had shown a similar inclination.

"However, after your treatment of Selina, I began to wonder if the list *was* a good thing. I hated to think a child of mine had become so pompous and judgmental, thinking himself better than everyone else, but when I thought on the matter further, I found I didn't really believe that of you. I think rather that your list was in the nature of a defense, a shield, if you will. So many young women had shown themselves attracted to you because of your fortune that you were determined not to give your love to a woman who might in turn prove unworthy. And I think that also accounted for your vehemence toward Selina when you thought you had been tricked after all."

"Mother, I know that you think I have treated Selina unfairly, and I realize she is blameless in this latest affair, but I am still not convinced that she did not set out to entrap me."

"Jeremy, I never knew you were such a poor judge of character. Although they do say love is blind, I have never heard it said it is deaf and dumb as well," Lady Kilbourne said, shaking her head in disbelief. "It is obvious to the meanest intelligence that Selina Dalton does not have a deceitful bone in her body. I have never met so sincere and honest a young lady. Her only fault in this affair lies in her association with Julia Thistlewaite. Now, *she's* a schemer if ever there was one."

Malcolm was silent for a moment, considering what his mother had said. "It is obvious that everyone else shares your opinion, but I was so worried that I was allowing her to make a fool of me. She is so outrageously beautiful, you know. I wanted to make sure I was allowing my head to rule me, and not my—"

"I grasp your meaning, Jeremy," Lady Kilbourne said, with a minatory glance at her son.

"I was going to say my heart, Mother," Malcolm said, the first hint of a smile showing on his face.

"Of course you were. That is what I thought as well," Lady Kilbourne said briskly, quickly changing the subject. "I know that it is difficult to let someone past the guard you've so carefully put up around your heart, but unless you do, you're in danger of losing Selina altogether. Love cannot be planned so carefully, my dear. It will stir things up a bit. That is part of its charm." Lady Kilbourne reached up to smooth her son's hair off of his forehead. Then she cleared her throat before saying, "So, what do you plan to do?"

"I do not know," Malcolm said, looking very vulnerable all of a sudden. "Do you have any suggestions?"

"I would suggest you find Miss Dalton immediately and tell her you've made a mistake."

"I do not think she will speak to me. She was very angry."

"Of course she was. But if you do not go to her now, I am quite sure she will find some way to leave Hadley Hall, and then you will never get this sorted out."

"You're right. I shall do so immediately," Malcolm said.

"Good. Because I would like to see your father again sometime before Michaelmas," Lady Kilbourne said, turning to leave the room. "I do not mind spending short periods away from him, you know, because it is only then that he realizes how fond he is of me, but if am away too long, there is always the danger he'll forget me entirely. Lord Cassidy, please do not keep Jeremy too long; I expect him to perform an errand for me before dinner," Lady Kilbourne said as she passed Cassie on her way out of the room.

Malcolm sat down at his desk and motioned to a chair in front of him. "If this traffic in and out of my library keeps up, I will have to replace the rug," he said.

Cassie would not sit but stood in front of the desk, staring determinedly down at Malcolm. "I have come to see if you intend to do the proper thing toward Miss Dalton," he said.

"I believe it is her father's place to do that," Malcolm said.

"It is the place of anyone concerned about her welfare, as I am. Because if you do not intend to follow through and marry her, I intend to," Cassie said.

"That is very gallant of you, Cassie, but unnecessary. I fully intend to marry Miss Dalton, if I can convince her to have me."

"I would not blame her for refusing. You have treated her deplorably. You couldn't have been more stupid if you had been a demon."

"Excuse me?" Malcolm asked, confused. "I wasn't aware that demons had a reputation for stupidity."

"Do not try to turn the subject. You've been acting like that Greek fellow you were dressed like the other night, Ademon. You know, here Miss Dalton is, hopelessly in love with you, and you're behaving as if you're sound asleep."

"Ah, I understand. You're referring to *Endymion*."

"Call him whatever you'd like. The point is, you have treated the girl unconscionably, and I do not intend to stand by and watch you do so any longer. We've always been friends, Jeremy, but I am afraid I cannot remain your friend if you continue to mistreat Miss Dalton."

Malcolm rose from the desk to clap Cassie on the shoulder. "Well said, old friend. I agree that I've behaved very badly indeed. And I intend to do something about it this instant." Malcolm left the room, and Cassie stood there, congratulating himself on the success of his lecture. He began to wonder if perhaps he had a future in the House of Lords after all. If he could just make heads or tails of those Corn Laws, he was sure he could write a speech that would change the country's economy. He envisioned himself standing before his peers, addressing them like that Antony fellow did in Shakespeare's play.

"'Friends, Romans, countrymen, lend me your ears,'" he quoted, pleased at the sound of it. Then he realized he could not say "Romans," and sat there for the next half hour trying to think of a fitting substitute. When he could not find a word that worked as well, he gave up the task, not too upset his political career had come to nothing after all.

Malcolm, who was unable to locate Selina anywhere else, realized that she must be in her bedroom. He knew it was not at all appropriate for him to talk to her there, but as she was already hopelessly compromised, he concluded it no longer mattered whether or not they paid strict attention to the proprieties. So he rapped lightly on the door to her bedroom, a little surprised when she told him to go away even before she knew it was he.

"Miss Dalton," he said, "I need to speak with you."

There was a short pause, and then Selina said without opening the door, "I believe you've said quite enough already."

"Please, Miss Dalton, *Selina*, I want to apologize," Malcolm said.

The door opened and Selina stood in front of him, her arms crossed in front of her. She did not appear to be in a very good mood. "I am waiting," she said.

"Surely you do not expect me to stand here in the hall where anyone might happen by," Malcolm protested when she made no move to let him in.

She stood watching him a moment and then preceded him into her chamber, leaving the door open behind her. "I hope if someone chances upon us you will remember that I preferred you to stay in the hall. I do not want to be accused once again of attempting to entrap you," Selina said.

Malcolm did not respond, his attention caught by the obvious signs that she had been packing. There were dresses piled on the bed and an open trunk on the floor. "What are you doing?" he asked her, staring around him in dismay.

"It is called packing," she said.

"But you cannot leave!"

"Why ever not? You cannot pretend that you will miss me. I was sure you would be eager to see the last of such an unsavory character as myself."

Malcolm winced. "That is why I am here. I wanted to tell you I was very wrong to accuse you of trickery. My mother was behind the events of this afternoon."

Selina's angry expression slipped for a moment, to be replaced by one of surprise. "Your mother locked us in the conservatory?" she asked. "But why?"

"She was determined to secure you as a daughter-in-law. She admires you very much."

"I am honored that your mother likes me, but I would

prefer she not demonstrate it in so unusual a manner," Selina said.

"She was afraid I would make a muddle of it on my own, I suppose, which I have," Malcolm said. "That is why I have come to beg your forgiveness."

It was a pity that Malcolm's demeanor did not lend itself to humble apologies. He looked the very antithesis of a 'beggar.' "How very noble of you," Selina replied.

"Why do I get the impression you are being insincere?" Malcolm asked.

"Forgive me, but it is a little difficult to be accused of participating in some heinous scheme to dupe someone one moment, and then not an hour later be told that all is well because you've discovered your *mother* was behind it. Did you proceed to wash your hands of her as well? The Honorable Jeremy Malcolm could not bear to associate with anyone who was less than perfect, even his own mother."

"Selina, you do not understand; I still want to marry you," Malcolm said.

Selina could not believe the gall of this man. "No, sir, you are the one who does not understand. I still do *not* want to marry you. Did you really believe you could say 'I'm sorry' and all the events of the last few days would be erased? I realize you are used to getting what you want, but even you must recognize it is not that easy."

"But what about your reputation? It has been irreparably besmirched."

"Hang my reputation! I would rather be considered a fallen woman—though that is quite an exaggeration of the facts of the matter—than to be placed in a relationship where I am not trusted. What if we were to marry and one day you found that your slippers were missing? I would probably be hauled before a magistrate and accused of theft!"

"I can assure you that would never happen. I realize that my behavior of the past few days has been offensive. No one regrets it more than I do," Malcolm said, reaching for Selina's hand. She quickly pulled away, and he realized that she was far too angry to hear his apologies. But he could not permit her to leave Hadley Hall. He had to find some way to convince her to stay at least a few more days.

"I understand why you feel you cannot accept my proposal, but please continue to accept my hospitality. Do not feel compelled to leave."

Selina calmed a little at his reasonable tone. "Thank you, sir, for extending the invitation, but I feel it would be best if I left as soon as possible."

"Selina—" Selina glared at him and Malcolm realized whatever tacit permission he'd been accorded to address her by her Christian name had been revoked. He corrected himself: "Miss Dalton, be reasonable. You may not be concerned about your reputation, but I do care about mine. If you leave and we are not engaged, people are bound to think I behaved dishonorably toward you. Why, Cassie has already threatened to end our friendship if I do not marry you. If you stay on for a few more days, perhaps a week, and we enter into a pretend engagement, then later we can say that you jilted me. That should salvage your reputation to some extent."

"Or even enhance it. I'll go down in history as the only woman to have refused you," Selina said, and her expression brightened a little. Malcolm found it extremely discouraging that the thought of jilting him was the only thing that could bring a smile to her face. But at least she appeared to be considering the idea. She was silent a moment longer, and Malcolm held his breath . . .

"And it would only be for a few days—" Selina began.

"I think a week would be better," Malcolm said, interrupting her.

"All of the guests are scheduled to leave in three days. I do not think our performance needs to extend past their departure," Selina said, looking suspiciously at Malcolm.

Malcolm hurried to dispel her suspicions. "You are right, of course. I had forgotten that was the date mentioned. So you will do it?"

"Only if it is made perfectly clear that *I* chose to jilt *you*," Selina said.

"Of course. And you'll behave as if we are engaged?" Malcolm asked.

"I will not deny it if asked, but do not expect me to play the adoring fiancée."

"Of course not, I do not expect it of you," Malcolm said. "Although if you could behave as if you do not find me utterly repulsive, that might make our engagement a little more believable."

"But I thought you could not abide deception? Surely you would not want me to prevaricate?" Selina asked, wide-eyed.

Malcolm realized the next three days were going to be more difficult than he could ever have imagined.

Not long after Malcolm left there was another knock at the door. Selina resisted the urge to again yell "Go away," remembering that she was now supposed to be a happily engaged woman. So she went to the door, only to find Julia in the process of opening it.

"Selina, I am so glad you and Mr. Malcolm have worked out all of your problems. I was absolutely consumed with guilt, but now I can be happy again," Julia said, following Selina into the room.

Selina was in the midst of returning her clothes to the closet. She continued with that task, while Julia made herself comfortable on the window seat. "I am overjoyed that you no longer have me on your conscience," Selina said.

"What are you doing?" Julia asked, ignoring her friend's sarcasm.

"I am unpacking."

"Unpacking? How can you be unpacking—we have been here for over a week. I do not understand," Julia said.

"Yes, well, I had begun to pack, but then changed my mind, and now I am unpacking."

"Why had you begun to pack? Surely you were not going to leave right after becoming engaged? I have to say, I am quite pleased with the way things turned out. I thought at first that I may have ruined your prospects, but now I think you have reason to be grateful to me."

This was too much for Selina to bear. "Before you begin congratulating yourself too enthusiastically, you should know that Mr. Malcolm and I are only pretending to be engaged until the house party ends, at which time I plan to jilt him." Selina smiled slightly. "You know, I think that is the only part of this whole affair that I will enjoy."

Julia sat up in her seat and stared at Selina in dismay. "What do you mean, pretending to be engaged? Why would you pretend? You appeared to be getting along rather well together in the fountain."

Selina blushed at the reference to her aquatic activities, busying herself with the remaining dresses on the bed. "Yes, well, that is what finally determined me against him. He had the gall to suggest that I had arranged the afternoon's events in order to entrap him."

"Did you?" Julia asked.

"Of course I did not!" Selina said, offended. "Lady Kilbourne did."

"Really? I would have never suspected it of her. She always behaves so properly. I find her a little intimidating, actually. I had wondered if Cassie was behind it, but it was executed so well I had to discount him immediately. If he had done it, *he* would have ended up in the fountain."

Selina found herself giggling at Julia's comment, much to her own surprise. She sobered almost immediately, throwing herself onto the bed and wailing, "Oh, why did I have to fall in love with such a man? He's so infuriating!"

"I'm sure I cannot say. Then again, I would have never expected to find myself attracted to Henry Ossory. He's so . . . *nice*," Julia said, wrinkling her nose in distaste.

"I wish my problem were that Malcolm is nice, but it is the exact opposite. You would not believe the things he said to me."

"But you said Lady Kilbourne locked you in the conservatory. Does Mr. Malcolm know?"

"Yes, he is the one who told me. And he apologized for his suspicions of me, and said he still wanted to marry me. But it is not enough, Julia. He's distrustful of me and he's being forced into marriage with me. That is not the foundation for a happy relationship."

"Does he know that you wanted to leave?"

"Yes, that is when he came up with the idea of the false betrothal. He said he did not want people to think he had behaved dishonorably toward me."

"I think that was an excuse to make you stay, Selina. It is not like any of us would have gossiped about the matter. No, I believe he is much more anxious for this match than you suppose."

"Do you really?" Selina asked hopefully.

"I do indeed. Which is not to say that he should not be allowed to suffer a little," Julia said with a wicked smile.

"Julia, perhaps it would be best if you did not interfere," Selina said, a little worried by that smile.

"Nonsense. Everything will be fine. Trust me."

Selina would as lief trust a snake, but she nodded meekly, having learned that it did not pay to argue with Julia.

16

It is to be wondered why Selina and Malcolm were feigning an engagement when practically the entire house party knew it to be a pretense. Malcolm had confided the truth to his mother, who had confided in Mrs. Dalton, who had confided in Mr. Dalton. Selina had of course told Julia, who had told Henry and Cassie. The only person who did not know what was transpiring was Mrs. Thistlewaite, who would not have cared anyway, as she was engrossed in a particularly challenging piece of needlework.

However, the entire party went out of their way to pretend they were totally unaware there was anything amiss with the engagement. At dinner it was all anyone spoke of and, upon retiring into the drawing room afterward, the conversation was still focused on the supposed nuptials, until Selina felt she would rather scream than answer another question about when the wedding was to be, and where, and who was to make up the bridal party.

Lady Kilbourne and Julia were having more fun than they could remember in their attempts to put Malcolm and Selina out of countenance. Lady Kilbourne was particularly successful when she suggested that Malcolm and Selina ride out in the morning so that Malcolm could introduce his affianced bride to his tenants.

Malcolm, who appreciated what his mother was trying to do, thought she was in danger of going too far. Selina was far from looking the part of the blissful bride, and looked particularly perturbed at Lady Kilbourne's suggestion.

"Perhaps it would be better if we took such a tour once the banns are published," Malcolm suggested.

"And have your tenants feel as if they were the last to know? I do not think that would serve at all," Lady Kilbourne protested. "No, it is better for you to go tomorrow."

Malcolm looked over at Selina with a shrug, as if to say he had tried, but there was no gainsaying his mother. Secretly, however, he was pleased. He figured the more times Selina was introduced as his fiancée the more real the notion would become to her, and the harder it would be for her to end the engagement. Malcolm suspected that was probably why his mother made the suggestion in the first place, and he began to feel a whole new respect for her. He also realized that his poor father had never really stood a chance.

He left Selina's side to walk to the tea tray, where he was joined by Julia. "So you and Selina are to make a match of it after all," she said.

"It does appear that way," Malcolm said.

Julia smiled at the way he phrased his response, which caused Malcolm to wonder what it was that made her grin so. "I am very pleased that you are to marry my friend," Julia said, "but I must tell you that there is one person who is still not reconciled to the match."

"Indeed? Who might that be?" Malcolm asked, hoping she would not say Selina.

"Why, Mr. Ossory, of course. You must have noticed how he admires her. He confided to me that he wishes she will cry off, for he still has hopes in that regard."

Malcolm looked over to where Selina was sitting just in time to see Henry approach her and take the seat Malcolm had just vacated. He had no way of knowing that Julia had arranged matters that way.

"I am sorry that Mr. Ossory still entertains hopes in that direction, because he is destined for disappointment," Malcolm said, looking quite fierce.

"I must admit I would be happier were he not to attain that particular goal," Julia said. "So I have come to warn you not to do anything foolish that might cause Selina to break the engagement, because then we will both have cause for regret."

Malcolm just nodded, still observing Henry and Selina, and Julia smiled, pleased to see him looking so tormented. She was less pleased when he walked briskly over to Selina and Henry, demanding his seat be returned to him and making it obvious he was angry.

Henry walked over to Julia's side, looking rather bewildered. "I swear, I do not know what is wrong with Malcolm. His mood seems irrationally violent. I had just gone over to speak to Miss Dalton as you suggested and he nearly bit my head off. I hope they work out their differences soon."

"Oh, he is merely jealous. I told him you still had hopes for a match with Selina and he is indulging in a fit of temper."

"You did what?" Henry asked, his voice louder than usual. When Julia noticed they had become the cynosure of all eyes, she quickly pulled him out the doors to the gardens.

"It is all perfectly harmless. I just wanted to be sure that he values Selina as he ought. I thought if he knew that you were waiting in the wings, he would be even less likely to allow Selina to break their engagement."

"Miss Thistlewaite, *Julia*, I have had it with you inventing stories and getting me involved in these silly schemes of yours."

Julia was surprised to see that Henry was really angry. "But, Henry," Julia said tentatively, looking at him to see if he objected to this use of his Christian name. She had thrilled to hear *her* name on *his* lips, even though he appeared to have said it in exasperation rather than fondness. When he did not object, she continued, "This is not a scheme; it's really very innocent. You don't even have to *do* anything. Although it might be a good idea if you showed Selina a *little* extra attention."

"You see! That is exactly what I mean. I refuse to pretend an attraction I do not feel, just because you've been fabricating stories."

"But it is not an attraction you do not feel. You *are* attracted to Selina."

"So now I am not even allowed to decide to whom I am attracted? The least you could do is allow me to decide that! Does *this* seem as though I am attracted to Selina Dalton?" Henry asked, and pulled Julia into his arms, where she was very thoroughly kissed. "Well?" he asked afterward, but in a completely different tone of voice than he had used previously.

"Henry," Julia said softly, still nestled in his arms, "I thought you were nice."

So Henry had no choice but to kiss her again, in a manner that was considerably naughtier than it was nice.

Things were not proceeding as well for the couple still in the drawing room. After Henry and Julia left the room, Selina turned to Malcolm and questioned his behavior toward Mr. Ossory.

"Yes, I am sure you would not want me behaving unkindly toward *Ossory*," Malcolm said, in a voice laden with significance.

"I do not want you behaving unkindly toward anyone," Selina said. "But particularly toward someone who is supposed to be your friend."

"Yes, he is *supposed* to be my friend, just as you are *supposed* to be my intended bride."

Selina looked at him in justifiable confusion. "I gather from your tone of voice I am expected to infer something from that statement, but I have no idea what you're talking about."

"I am sure you do not," Malcolm said, still in that sarcastic tone. "You are just biding your time, aren't you? You are just waiting until you can jilt me so you can announce your real engagement to Henry Ossory."

"My engagement to Henry Ossory?" Selina started to laugh. "Mr. Malcolm, we've been through all this already. Mr. Ossory no longer has any interest in me other than that of a friend. I am beginning to believe he is forming an attachment to Julia after all, poor man."

"Miss Thistlewaite just told me—" Malcolm began, only to realize that the other inhabitants of the drawing room were paying much more attention to his and Selina's conversation than they were to their own pursuits. A whist game that had begun between Cassie, Lady Kilbourne, and Mr. and Mrs. Dalton had ceased altogether, and even Mrs. Thistlewaite had looked up from her needlework.

"Excuse us for a moment," Malcolm said, pulling Selina through the French doors that Julia and Henry had exited a few minutes earlier. Once on the terrace they were confronted with the sight of Julia and Henry locked in a passionate embrace, barely ten feet away.

"You were saying?" Selina asked Malcolm softly, so as not to disturb the kissing couple.

Malcolm shook his head in disbelief. "I will never believe another word out of that woman's mouth. I wonder if Ossory knows what he's getting into."

Selina glanced back at the couple. "He does not appear to mind."

She started to return to the drawing room when Malcolm stopped her with a hand on her arm. "Wait," he whispered. "Why don't we take a walk in the gardens? They appear to have had quite an effect on our friends."

"Thank you for the offer, but you forget that we are not truly engaged. And you must have a care for your reputation," Selina said, wriggling out of his grasp and returning through the French doors into the drawing room. But Malcolm was relieved to see that she was smiling.

"No, I have not forgotten we are not truly engaged. That's what I was proposing to remedy," Malcolm said aloud, still facing the doors. He turned back toward Julia and Henry, determined to interrupt their rendezvous. It was unfair of them to be so cozily entwined while he was out there alone. He walked closer to them, clearing his throat loudly.

Julia and Henry did not spring apart guiltily, as occurs in all the best novels, but they did separate long enough to notice Malcolm standing there, glaring at them. Malcolm hoped Julia was blushing, but it was impossible to tell by moonlight.

"Jeremy, old chap," Henry said. "I noticed that you and Miss Dalton had come onto the terrace but I was hoping you'd appreciate our desire for privacy."

"Henry, I must warn you that the woman you are embracing is a lying, deceiving hussy," Malcolm said, slowly and clearly.

Julia gasped, and looked to Henry to come to her defense. "I know all that, my friend," Henry said, "but I thank you for the warning just the same."

Julia began struggling to get out of Henry's embrace. "Why, you—you dastardly knave, you scoundrel, you—"

"Hush," Henry said, ignoring Julia's efforts to free herself. "You didn't allow me to finish. I was going to tell him I plan on devoting my life to keeping those nasty habits of yours in check."

Malcolm could not see how that statement could possibly be construed as a compliment, but it seemed to have the appropriate effect, for Julia was no longer attempting to leave Henry's embrace. "You do?" she asked.

"I do indeed," Henry said. "In fact, I positively look forward to it."

"Oh, Henry!" Julia replied, staring up at him adoringly.

As it was obvious Henry was about to initiate another kiss, Malcolm gave up on attempting to reason with him and returned to the drawing room.

Selina retired to her chamber directly after leaving Malcolm on the terrace, more cheerful than she'd been in days. She was happy for her friend Julia, of course, but she was even more pleased that Malcolm was jealous. She doubted he would have been so angry with Henry if he was not a *little* in love with her. For the first time since that dreadful masquerade ball she allowed herself to become optimistic about her future. She lay on her bed, staring at the ceiling, saying aloud, "Mrs. Selina Malcolm, Mrs. Jeremy Malcolm," and laughing over how silly she was being. She shivered at the thought of receiving more kisses from Malcolm, and thought she might have enjoyed some that very evening if she hadn't refused his offer to walk in the gardens. Her imaginings took her to the altar and beyond, but none of her thoughts were of Mr. Malcolm's estate or his riches. No, it was the gentleman himself she dreamed about, and if some of those dreams brought a flush to her cheeks and a fluttering to her stomach, who could fault her for dreaming?

After some time spent that way, she heard a knock on the door and Julia joined her, to give her all the details of her own courtship and engagement. The two girls were up until the wee hours of the morning, whispering and talking and giggling, and entering into arguments over which of their beaux was the worthier.

Selina was still in a good mood when she awoke the next morning, and quickly changed into her dark green habit in order to go riding with Malcolm. She joined the others in the breakfast room, and pretended not to notice when most of her fellow diners watched her and Malcolm like they were animals in a menagerie.

Later, while she and Malcolm were riding, she asked him if he'd told anyone about their false betrothal.

"Only my mother," he said. "Why? Did you tell anyone?"

"I only told Julia. But I felt at breakfast like some of the others might know as well."

"Really? What gave you that impression?" Malcolm asked, though he had formed the same opinion himself.

"The way they were observing us," Selina said, and shrugged. "Oh, well, it is probably my imagination."

"I am sure it is," Malcolm said, worried lest she refuse to carry on the pretense and leave before the three days were up. He introduced her to everyone he saw that morning as "Miss Selina Dalton, my intended wife." When he even stopped a passing farmer to introduce her, Selina protested.

"Malcolm, I am sure that man does not care that I am your fiancée. He is not one of your tenants. I do not think he is even from this county," she said once the farmer had driven on.

"That is true. I thought I recognized him, but it's obvious I mistook him for someone else."

Selina just smiled and shook her head. She was not going to protest too much. She had to admit she liked the way it sounded when Malcolm performed the introductions. Almost as if he were proud that she was his future wife, real or imagined.

Malcolm *was* proud of Selina. She was so beautiful, so kind, so much the lady, that he was very pleased to be able to tell people she was his affianced bride. And he was determined to ensure the match was as real in her mind as it was in his. Half of the three days were already gone, so he hadn't much time to lose. When he reached up to help her from her horse, he almost told her of his feelings then. She was looking down at him, a sweet smile on her face. His hands were around her waist, and he had an overwhelming desire to pull her into his arms, a desire that he thought he saw reflected in her eyes. He was about to act on that desire, when a groom suddenly appeared and he was forced to release her. She seemed as disappointed at the interruption as he. He had no other choice but to escort her into the house.

Malcolm was correct in thinking that Selina was disappointed at the interruption. She had thought herself close to being kissed very soundly, and was irritated that they were always interrupted at the most inopportune moments. She returned to her chamber to change into an afternoon gown, and stood in front of the closet for quite some time, trying to decide which gown would incite Malcolm to declare his undying love for her.

Selina was still standing in front of the closet, dressed in her riding habit when she heard a knock at the door. "Come in," she called absently, still staring into the closet. She thought it was probably Mary, come to help her dress. She did not even turn around, and so was taken completely by surprise when Cassie said, "Miss Dalton, you must come with me at once."

"What?" she said, turning to look at him. He appeared extremely agitated; he was nearly wringing his hands in worry. "Is something the matter?"

"It most certainly is. I haven't got time to tell you all the details; we must go down to the stables immediately." He put his hand under her elbow and began leading her out of the room and down the stairs. Cassie was considerably taller than Selina, and she was hampered by the long skirts of her habit, so she was distracted from questioning him too intently. She was focused instead on trying to keep from tripping on her skirts and breaking her neck.

"Cassie, could you stop pushing me? I am about to tumble headlong down the stairs," Selina said in exasperation.

"We must hurry," he replied, leading her through the front entry hall and down the steps. A curricle was standing in front of the hall with a groom holding the horses.

"Why must we hurry? You have not told me what is wrong. Is one of the horses ill?" Selina knew Cassie was generally more concerned about horses than people, although what he thought she could do to help she couldn't fathom.

"No, it's much worse than that. Julia's run off."

"What do you mean 'run off'? Where would she go?"

"I don't know. It's probably some scheme of hers. But if we don't get her back soon, she's going to ruin her chances with Ossory. He doesn't think too highly of her scheming." As Cassie was talking, he was urging Selina into a curricle. She had no desire to go anywhere, particularly not on some wild-goose chase searching for Julia, but her protests went unheeded, and before she realized it Cassie was directing his horses down the drive and onto the main road.

"If you don't know where Julia is, where are we going?"

"To an inn in Tunbridge Wells. She mentioned it last night. I think that's probably where she's gone."

"But why? She spoke to me last night and she said nothing of going anywhere. Why would she go off by herself and risk ruining her reputation when she's so close to becoming engaged to Mr. Ossory?"

"Why are you asking so many questions?" Cassie said, looking sulky. "I told you I don't know. I've never been able to figure out what Julia's thinking. I just know she's always thinking up stupid schemes to make my life difficult."

Selina had to acknowledge this was true, but she still thought it strange that Julia hadn't intimated anything of the sort in their conversation last night. But Cassie was evidently not in the mood to talk so she stopped questioning him. She did notice however, that he had not taken the road to Tunbridge Wells. He was going in the direction of London.

"Cassie, you're going the wrong way," she told him.

"Eh? No, I don't think so. Why don't you look at the pretty flowers?"

"You are definitely going the wrong way. This road goes to London. You should have turned back there for Tunbridge Wells. I saw the sign."

"I know where I'm going. By Jove, look at the pretty rosebush," he said, pointing at a rhododendron.

Selina was frustrated beyond belief. She could not imagine why she'd let this yahoo ever talk her into going anywhere with him. She reached over and grabbed his hands that held the reins and pulled as hard as she could.

"Selina!" Cassie yelled at her as the horses reared back in confusion. "Are you trying to kill us? Don't do that." Selina knew this was her only chance to escape. The ground looked awfully far away, but so was London, and she had no intention of spending hours on a journey there with Cassie. So before the horses had a chance to resume their previous speed, she stood up in the curricle, preparing to jump.

"What are you doing?" Cassie shouted, pulling the horses

to a halt with one hand and grabbing the back of Selina's dress with the other. She was extremely relieved she hadn't had to jump while they were moving. Now that she was standing up, the ground looked even farther away.

"I have no intention of going with you to London, Cassie. So please explain to me right now what all of this is about."

Cassie sighed, running a hand through his already thoroughly disheveled hair. "Women!" he said disgustedly. "You can never just do as you're told."

"From what I recall, you haven't *told* me anything," Selina said, resuming her seat.

"It's for your own good, don't you see? I left a note. The others think we're eloping. I told them that since Malcolm wasn't prepared to do the honorable thing, I was going to."

"You did what?" Selina asked in disbelief. "Why?"

"Julia told me the engagement was just a farce. I thought Malcolm needed some help coming to the sticking point. Now that he knows Ossory is interested in Julia, you needed someone else to make him jealous. I was happy to oblige."

"Did Julia and Henry know about this, or was it your idea entirely?"

"It was entirely my own idea," Cassie said, looking smug.

"Well, while I appreciate your concern, I hardly think abducting me in the middle of the afternoon will induce Malcolm to propose. He'll probably just think it's another attempt to deceive him, which will have the effect of making him distrust me again."

"Dash it, I never thought of that."

"Yes, well, there's no harm done. Why don't we just turn around and go back," Selina said.

Cassie looked a little disappointed at the suggestion. He had thought participating in an elopement, even a false one, was a dashing thing to do. He had no desire to return meekly to Hadley Hall and spend the afternoon drinking tea in the drawing room. He was a man of action.

Selina, sensing his disappointment, said, "Perhaps you could teach me to drive your curricle on the way home."

Cassie perked up a little at her remark. He could envision himself riding up the drive to Hadley Hall, his arms masterfully around Selina as she held the reins. Malcolm would have to sit up and take notice then. "All right. You need to learn. Or else you're going to end up killing someone. The first lesson is never to yank the reins when someone else is driving," he told Selina, while racking his brain to figure out a way to guarantee Malcolm would see them together.

17

Cassie could not believe his good fortune. As luck would have it, Malcolm exited the house just as Cassie and Selina started up the drive. Selina had progressed to the point in their lessons where she was fully able to hold the reins without Cassie's help, but when he saw Malcolm off in the distance Cassie immediately threw his arms around Selina in a tight embrace, placing his hands on hers.

Selina was startled by this sudden move on Cassie's part. She twisted her body, trying to put distance between herself and Cassie. "What are you doing?" she asked, turning to look at him.

"Never mind," Cassie said, who was peering in Malcolm's direction trying to see his reaction. "Just keep driving."

"I can't drive when you're on top of me like this. You're pulling the horses in the wrong direction. Cassie!" she yelled, as she looked forward and realized they were headed directly for the lake.

Cassie turned at Selina's scream and pulled hard on the reins. He was able to turn the horses at the last moment so the curricle did not enter the water, but the wheel sunk into the damp ground at the edge of the lake and tipped sideways, and Selina and Cassie were tossed into the murky water.

The water was shallow and they were not traveling very fast so Selina was not hurt, but she was shocked to be suddenly capsized into the lake. It was muddy where she landed, and she was bogged down even further by her long skirt. She attempted to stand and tripped and fell down backward, landing on her bottom. Cassie was a foot or so away, and she realized it was his leg she'd tripped over. He hadn't attempted to move; apparently he had still not recovered from the shock of finding himself in the lake. Before she could make a second attempt to get up, Malcolm appeared on the scene.

He observed them in silence for a moment, his expression serious. "Is this some sort of bizarre mating ritual with you, Selina?" Malcolm asked.

"That is not funny in the least," Selina replied, struggling to get up.

"I was not attempting to be funny. I am not at all in the

mood for jokes, having discovered the woman to whom I'm engaged ran off with another man."

Selina ceased her struggling, looking at Malcolm in disbelief. "You cannot believe I would actually elope with Cassie?"

Cassie took umbrage at her tone. "There's no need to be insulting. Plenty of young ladies would jump at the chance," he muttered, but was ignored by both Selina and Malcolm.

"I must admit I thought it far-fetched at first, but then to see you drive up practically in his arms, well, what was I to think?"

"Exactly," Cassie offered, grinning at the success of his plot, and he was again ignored.

"That your addlepated friend had abducted me and was intent on dumping me into the lake," Selina said.

"That last bit wasn't part of the plan, actually," Cassie said.

"Oh, please be quiet, both of you, and somebody help me out of this lake."

Malcolm was instantly remorseful. He hadn't really believed Selina had eloped with Cassie—the idea was laughable, of course—but he couldn't help feeling pangs of jealousy when he saw *his* woman in the arms of another man. He knew he was acting positively primeval but he couldn't seem to help himself. If Selina didn't consent to marry him soon, he was sure to start conversing in grunts while beating any man who looked in her direction with a club.

He stepped as close as he could to the water, reaching out a hand to Selina. He was so busy berating himself for his lack of chivalry that he completely missed her wicked smile and the mischievous gleam that lit her eyes before she pulled him in.

Malcolm was shocked to find himself on his hands and knees in the cold water, with Selina's laughing face just inches from his own. "Why, you little vixen!" he said, reaching for her with his muddy hands.

Selina's laugh turned into a little scream, but Malcolm merely splashed some water in her face and pretended he was going to pull her under. When he became aware that Cassie was laughing at him as well, Malcolm splashed him for good measure. Fairly soon the three of them were in a wholesale water fight while Selina giggled and shrieked, totally oblivious to the fact that they'd attracted an audience.

It was not until Lady Kilbourne very calmly said, "I see that we are going to need more towels," that they stopped their horseplay and looked around.

Lady Kilbourne was standing at the banks of the lake, along with Mr. and Mrs. Dalton and Julia and Henry. They were watching the threesome in the water with varying expressions of amusement and dismay. Lady Kilbourne broke the silence again to ask, "I know, Jeremy, that you and Selina are engaged, but who's going to do the proper thing for Lord Cassidy?"

Selina quickly cleaned up and started down the stairs to join the others. She was met at the foot of the stairs by Malcolm, who told her that since Cassie's note had been delivered directly to him no one else knew of the aborted elopement, and that they should just tell everyone that Cassie was giving Selina a driving lesson when the accident occurred that launched them into the lake.

"Did Cassie tell you why he attempted to elope with me?" Selina asked a little fearfully. She did not want Malcolm to know it had been another ploy to entrap him.

"He was overcome by your beauty, of course. What other reason could there be?" Malcolm answered lightly. Selina thought that he must have figured out the true reason but he did not seem bothered by it. It appeared as if he was finally beginning to trust her.

Before Malcolm could say anything else they were interrupted, and so they joined the others for luncheon.

The entire party was gathered in the drawing room after luncheon when Malcolm decided it was time to make his move. Turning to Selina, he asked if she would care to join him for a walk in the gardens. He was surprised to see his mother vehemently shaking her head no, just as Selina was nodding her head yes.

As he excused himself from Selina to go speak to his mother, he heard Mrs. Thistlewaite say, "Selina, dear, perhaps you'd do better to stay away from any bodies of water on your walk, considering those other unfortunate incidents. You know best, of course, but be careful not to get too close."

He did not hear Selina's reply, as he had reached his mother's side and she'd begun speaking, but he did hear a hastily suppressed snicker from Julia.

"Jeremy, dear, what are you about to do?" Lady Kilbourne asked her son.

"I am going to propose to Selina. Properly, this time."

Lady Kilbourne looked dismayed. "Jeremy, I don't think you've thought this out sufficiently. You can't just walk Selina out on the terrace and spring this on her, particularly after what has passed so far. You need a grand gesture, some romantic deed that conveys how much you love her." Lady Kilbourne paused, her finger on her chin. "Maybe you could compose a song," she finally suggested.

"Mother, I am not composing a song, and I'm not going to waste any more time with elaborate strategies when the girl I love is leaving my house the day after tomorrow, and I may lose whatever chance I have. Now, I appreciate all of your help thus far, but I can handle it on my own from this point forward."

"I must admit I have not been too impressed with your wooing ability thus far, but if you're certain this is the best way to go about it, I suppose you're right to trust your instincts." Lady Kilbourne did not sound very convinced.

"I appreciate the encouragement," Malcolm said, walking away from her.

During Malcolm's hushed conversation with his mother on one side of the drawing room, Mrs. Dalton had approached Selina on the other side.

"Selina, I need to tell you something before you walk with Mr. Malcolm," she said.

"Yes, Mama?"

Mrs. Dalton looked a little uncomfortable. "Now, dear, I know that you and Mr. Malcolm say that you are engaged, but Lady Kilbourne told me, in the strictest confidence, of course, that it is actually a pretense and that you refused his proposal. Now, don't be upset with her," Mrs. Dalton said as Selina started to speak, "she thought that I should know, and I think that she was right to tell me. I rather wondered that you did not tell me yourself." Mrs. Dalton held up her hand when Selina would have spoken again. "It's all right; your father and I discussed it and decided you were trying to spare our feelings—"

"'Your father'!" Selina repeated, finally able to interject a comment. "Papa knows as well?"

"I couldn't very well keep this kind of information from him. You mightn't have felt any compunction at doing so, but . . . at any rate," Mrs. Dalton continued, when it was obvious Selina was growing impatient, "I wanted to counsel you to accept Mr. Malcolm if he should propose again. I know that you admire him, so I cannot quite understand why you did not accept his first proposal. I realize some ladies may consider it fashionable to reject a gentleman's first proposal, but I must admit I didn't expect that sort of behavior from you. And if you reject another proposal, there may not be a third."

"I have every intention of accepting this time, Mama, so do not worry yourself on that score," Selina told her.

"Wonderful!" Mrs. Dalton said. "Then I have nothing left to say except I hope you enjoy your walk, and whatever you do, do not allow Mr. Malcolm to coerce you into the water."

It was unfortunate that Malcolm returned to Selina's side in time to hear Mrs. Dalton's last comment, but he manfully restrained himself from acknowledging it. With his most wooden expression, he turned to Selina and offered his arm. "Shall we go?"

They had turned to leave the room when Cassie surprised everyone by saying, "It's a nice day for a walk, by Jove. I think I will join you."

Malcolm turned to glare at his friend. "You were not invited."

Cassie was pleased at the success of his strategy. It was obvious Malcolm was fairly eaten up with jealousy. But Cassie thought he still needed a little further encouragement. "I daresay I can walk if I'd like. This is not a ball; I didn't think I'd need a formal invitation. What are you winking for, Malcolm? Do you have something in your eye?"

Julia came to Malcolm's rescue before he could respond, much to his surprise. "Cassie, please be quiet. It is obvious that Mr. Malcolm and Selina do not wish company on their walk." Before Malcolm could thank her for her kind interference, she rose from her seat next to Henry to walk over to Malcolm and say in an aside which was perfectly audible to Selina: "If you are taking Selina away in order to propose to her, I think I owe it to her as her friend to warn her of your less desirable qualities, as you were kind enough to do for Henry last night."

Malcolm had reached the limit of his endurance. In a tightly controlled voice that still managed to convey his frustration, he announced to all those in the room, "Would you all please allow me a moment's privacy so that I may be permitted to propose to my fiancée?"

Into the short silence that followed Malcolm's painful entreaty a new voice said, "I would think if the lady is your fiancée, you would have already accomplished that particular endeavor."

Standing on the threshold of the drawing room was an elegant gray-haired gentleman.

"Lord Kilbourne," Lady Kilbourne said, "this is a most pleasant surprise."

Lord Kilbourne approached his wife and raised her hand to his lips. "My dear, I had hoped it might be."

"Did you bring Robert and my so-charming daughter-in-law with you?" Lady Kilbourne asked him.

"No, I did not," her husband said.

"You are the most thoughtful of husbands," Lady Kilbourne told him.

It was obvious that Malcolm and Selina could not leave for a walk when Malcolm's father had just arrived, so Malcolm gritted his teeth and performed the introductions.

"I am not by nature superstitious," Malcolm whispered to Selina once the introductions had been made, "but I am beginning to wonder if an evil Fate is conspiring against us."

"I think the problem is not those who are conspiring against us, but rather those who are conspiring for us," Selina whispered back, and Malcolm laughed.

Selina was not too disappointed by the events of the afternoon. Of course, she would have preferred some privacy with Malcolm, but as Malcolm had very publicly announced his intention of proposing to her, there was no doubt in her mind that their false engagement had become very real. And as Malcolm had also retained her hand in a tight grip and showed no signs of leaving her side, she was about as content as one could be who had not yet heard a formal declaration of her beloved's intentions.

18

*I*t was not until after dinner that Selina and Malcolm managed to enjoy a little privacy together. At that time Malcolm escorted Selina through the French doors that led to the terrace with nary an objection from anyone.

"You will observe that I did not suggest we walk to the lake, a pond, the conservatory, or any other location where there might exist a body of water," Malcolm told Selina.

Selina giggled but could manage no other response, as she was suddenly overcome with shyness. She found she could not even meet Malcolm's gaze, but stood silently, her head lowered, her fingers nervously fiddling with a ribbon on her dress.

"Selina," Malcolm said, putting his finger under her chin and raising her head so that she was looking at him.

"I would like to offer an explanation for the deplorable way I treated you when I discovered Julia's little plot." He laughed a little nervously. "Actually, that is not at all what I would like to do, particularly when you are standing so close, but that is what you deserve to hear."

"I think I understand," Selina said, lifting her hand to touch his face. "It must not be easy to trust someone when you've been the victim of so much deceit for so long."

"That is part of the reason, but it is not the entire reason. To tell you the truth, I was relieved to find an excuse to discredit you, as curious as that seems. There is a certain feeling of . . . insecurity in loving someone. I had guarded myself from that sort of vulnerability for so long that I was petrified to let someone so close to me. Then, when I found an excuse not to let you in, I leapt at it. It was easier for me to think that you were like all the others than to allow you to disrupt my life. It was my mother who finally explained to me that love *is* disruptive."

"You make it sound like a disorder of the bowels or a carriage accident," Selina said.

Malcolm shook his head. "And my mother accuses *me* of being unromantic. Please remember that I did not introduce intestinal disorders into the midst of a marriage proposal."

"Oh, there is no need for you to propose. After hearing you introduce me for the tenth time as your intended bride, I no longer doubted it was true."

"So that little strategy of mine worked, did it?"

"Little strategy?" Selina drew back from Malcolm, her hands on her hips. "I no longer wonder you thought me capable of all kinds of treachery, when it is obvious that you yourself indulged in a number of different schemes. False betrothals, lies and subterfuge, tricks with your handkerchief."

"I must admit that last one was my favorite. Too bad I don't happen to have a wet handkerchief handy now," Malcolm said with a wicked smile before drawing her into an embrace that proved such trickery was really not necessary.

"Selina," he said a few minutes later, "you are distracting me from my goal. I am supposed to be proposing right now."

"I told you it was pointless. The wedding is already planned. I may as well continue to . . . distract you," Selina suggested, drawing his head back toward hers.

Malcolm removed her hands from around his neck, holding them firmly away from him. "As tempting a suggestion as that is, I insist on being allowed to propose. I do not want it thrown in my face every time we have an argument that you did not even receive a proper proposal."

"My dear Jeremy, I hope you're not suggesting this is a *proper* proposal," Selina said, having managed to free her hands and insinuate her way back into his embrace.

"Get away from me, woman," Malcolm said a few kisses later. "This is not at all the behavior I would have expected from a vicar's daughter." He staggered away from Selina, holding his hand out when she would have come to stand next to him again. "No, you must stay at least three feet away. I cannot guarantee your safety if you come any closer."

Selina stopped three feet away from him. "I am listening, Jeremy. I have just realized that this may be my last opportunity to hear a marriage proposal, proper or not."

Malcolm found that he could not bear to be that far away and moved closer, grabbing Selina's hands. "Selina, you are everything I've ever looked for in a woman, everything I could ever desire in a wife. *You* are the 'chief happiness that this world affords,' to misquote Johnson. I would be the happiest of men if you would consent to marry me."

"Oh, Jeremy, that was beautiful. I am so glad you insisted on it," Selina said, carrying his hand to her face.

"Selina, it isn't over yet. You have to accept."

"Oh, forgive me. Of course I will marry you. It is all I ever wanted from the time I first saw you in the library at Mrs. Harrington's ball. I suppose I owe you an explanation for my behavior as well."

"That is not necessary—" Malcolm started to say, before Selina interrupted him, placing her hand over his mouth.

"No, I want to get this sorted out once and for all. When I first came to town and Julia proposed that I take part in her scheme to humiliate you, I was not at all fond of the idea, but I truly believed it would come to naught, so I agreed. Julia really left me no other choice, and I was sure such a fastidious gentleman as she described would have no interest in me anyway. So I played along, but after actually making your acquaintance, I did try to withdraw from the game. Julia was very displeased with me, and tried to convince me that you deserved such treatment. So I tried another method: I tried to fail one of the qualifications on your list. I claimed not to have any musical talent."

"Ah. So that is why you behaved in so confusing a manner the night of the Thistlewaites' dinner party," Malcolm said.

"It did not work, obviously, but you have to believe I wanted nothing to do with Julia's scheme. When she insisted again that I take a part in it after we came to Hadley Hall, I positively refused. Julia was quite upset by my refusal, to say the least, and forged ahead with a plan of her own."

"I had guessed something of the sort, Selina, and I apologize for ever distrusting you."

Malcolm started to pull her back into his arms, and then stopped, reaching into his jacket. "Wait, I almost forgot. I wanted you to see this," he said, pulling out a piece of paper.

"What is it?" Selina asked, looking at it. "Oh, no, don't tell me this is your infamous list."

"No, it is not. It is a new list that I composed two days ago, when I realized what I really desired in a wife."

Selina began to read, but was only able to see the first three items before her eyes filled with tears. She read:

Is perfectly imperfect.

Makes me laugh.

Forgives me for being a misguided idiot.

They returned to the drawing room once Selina had composed herself. Malcolm cleared his throat, asked for everyone's attention, and announced that Selina had done him the honor of accepting his hand in marriage. There were some murmured congratulations, and then everyone returned to their previous occupations.

"Did everyone hear me?" Malcolm asked, looking at Selina in some confusion.

"Yes, dear, we know. You're engaged. You told us so two days ago," his mother said. "Now please sit down."

"No, we're really engaged this time."

"You were really engaged two days ago, old boy, you just didn't realize it," Henry told him. "But I would like to take this opportunity to let everyone know that Mrs. Thistlewaite has consented to grant me her daughter's hand, and we will also be getting married," Henry said, raising Julia's hand to his lips.

There was an excited babble of congratulations when Henry made his announcement, causing Malcolm and Selina to realize that they were already considered passé. Still, they congratulated their friends wholeheartedly, Selina hugging Julia.

"I am so happy for you," she said.

"Thank you, Selina. I have been thinking that since

Henry and I will most likely be standing up at your wedding, and you and Malcolm will be standing up for us, that we should all just be married together. What do you think?" Julia asked.

Selina saw her fiancé vigorously shaking his head from where he stood behind Julia. "I am not sure that a double wedding would be a good idea," Selina said.

"Oh, Selina, do not be such a namby-pamby," Julia told her.

19

*O*f course Julia got her way, and the wedding was scheduled for an early autumn day some few months later, with Mr. Dalton to preside over the ceremony. Julia had at first wanted a society wedding in London, but Henry was able to convince her otherwise, even when Selina and Malcolm failed.

Gertie was invited, and Selina intended to introduce her to a vulgar relation of Malcolm's whom she had met only recently. Selina was quite pleased when she found out that she was not the only one who had embarrassing family connections, and she teased Malcolm quite mercilessly about it, even telling him that she was unsure if the marriage could proceed in the face of this shocking revelation.

Lady Kilbourne was present when Selina was teasing

Malcolm about his cousin, and she added her bit as well. "I do not know why Jeremy pretended to be superior in that regard. One of his uncles was sent away with a keeper to a remote Cornwall property because he was always inebriated. Any attempt to sober him up always failed, and when he appeared at a dinner party having forgotten that he was . . . underdressed for the occasion, if you catch my meaning, we gave up on him altogether. He quite happily drank himself to death, although Lord Kilbourne did insist that we visit him twice a year before he died. That was quite unpleasant, I can assure you. He was unused to feminine company and was always overly affectionate in his dealings with me. And he insisted on calling me Kitty, no matter how many times I explained to him that was not my name."

"You are making that up," Malcolm said to his mother.

Lady Kilbourne looked surprised. "Indeed I am not. You were four when he died, so of course you would not remember him. And he is not the kind of relative one brags about." Lady Kilbourne turned to address Selina, who was struggling to keep from giggling. "My dear, it is not too late to reconsider. You have yet to meet your future sister-in-law, you know."

"I thank you for your concern, ma'am, but I am not as fastidious as Jeremy."

"And it is a good thing, too," Lady Kilbourne said. "You might not have consented to marry him if you had been."

Malcolm looked at his mother reproachfully. "Are you quite finished tearing my character to shreds in front of my fiancée? Or do you have any of my childish misdeeds you'd like to bring to her attention?"

"I am sure you have Selina telling you a thousand times a day how wonderful you are. It does you no harm to hear otherwise," Lady Kilbourne told her son.

"Well, she's only told me about nine hundred times to-day, so if you would give us a little privacy, I'm due to hear more," Malcolm said to his mother, motioning her toward the door.

Lady Kilbourne rose from where she'd been sitting, saying if her company was so unwelcome, she would go in search of Lord Kilbourne. "Because he has yet to tell me even once today how wonderful I am," she said on her way out of the room.

Malcolm barely waited for her to exit before scooping Selina into his arms and twirling her around the room. "Jeremy," Selina protested breathlessly. "What are you doing?"

Malcolm did not answer her, but kissed her instead, until she was even more breathless. "My mother was right, you know. If you had any sense at all you would realize you could do much better. I don't even meet the qualifications on my own list."

"Do you mean you have vulgar relations *and* that you have no musical talent?" Selina asked, wide-eyed. "We must call off the wedding immediately."

"I would not say I have *no* musical talent," Malcolm said.

"Well, you may not say so, but I heard you sing at church yesterday," Selina said.

"Wretch," Malcolm said, and hugged her tighter. "Perhaps I should not have mentioned the list after all."

"No, it is good that I know what I am getting into before we are irrevocably tied. I am beginning to see the value in these lists of yours," Selina said, drawing away from Malcolm and looking thoughtful.

"The whole thing was a horrid idea," Malcolm said, trying to pull Selina back into his arms.

"But I would really like to know what you think of the Corn Laws," Selina said, her expression solemn, but with laughter lurking in her eyes. "I have begun to realize that you are not serious enough, which augurs an unsteadiness of character."

"You have been speaking to Cassie," Malcolm said. "Has every stupid thing I've said or done been announced to the entire world?"

"Perhaps I can borrow the list Julia gave you while pretending to be me," Selina said, ignoring Malcolm's remark. "You would not still happen to have a copy, would you?"

"My dear girl," Malcolm said, beginning to look fierce, "I am done with all lists but one. It is a list of things that need to be done, and at the present moment there is one item that heads the list. Unfortunately, it has to wait until our wedding night."

Selina smiled up at Malcolm. "That sounds like your most interesting list yet."

Jeremy Malcolm's Requirements for a Wife

1. Amiable & even-tempered
2. Handsome of countenance & figure
3. Candid, truthful & guileless
4. Converses in a sensible fashion
5. Educates herself by extensive reading
6. A forgiving nature
7. Charitable & altruistic
8. Graceful & well-mannered
9. Possesses musical or artistic talent
10. Has genteel relations from good society

Photo by Jonathan Allain

Suzanne Allain is a screenwriter who lived in New York and Beijing before returning to her hometown of Tallahassee, Florida, where she lives with her husband. She makes frequent visits to Los Angeles for work, but one of her most memorable trips was to London to see her script *Mr. Malcolm's List: Overture* being filmed.

Connect Online

🐦 SuzanneAllain
📷 Suzanne.Allain

Do you love historical fiction?

Want the chance to hear news about your favourite authors (and the chance to win free books)?

Suzanne Allain
Mary Balogh
Lenora Bell
Charlotte Betts
Jessica Blair
Manda Collins
Grace Burrowes
Evie Dunmore
Lynne Francis
Pamela Hart
Elizabeth Hoyt
Eloisa James
Lisa Kleypas
Jayne Ann Krentz
Sarah MacLean
Terri Nixon
Julia Quinn

Then visit the Piatkus website
www.yourswithlove.co.uk

And follow us on Facebook and Instagram
www.facebook.com/yourswithlovex | @yourswithlovex

PIATKUS